UNICORNS

The Myths, Legends, & Lore

SKYE ALEXANDER

adamsmedia
Avon, Massachusetts

Published by
Adams Media, a division of F+W Media, Inc.
57 Littlefield Street, Avon, MA 02322. U.S.A.
www.adamsmedia.com

ISBN 10: 1-4405-9053-2
ISBN 13: 978-1-4405-9053-5
eISBN 10: 1-4405-9054-0
eISBN 13: 978-1-4405-9054-2

Printed in the United States of America.

10   9   8   7   6   5   4   3   2   1

Library of Congress Cataloging-in-Publication Data

Alexander, Skye.
    Unicorns / Skye Alexander.
        pages cm
    Includes bibliographical references.
    ISBN 978-1-4405-9053-5 (pob) -- ISBN 1-4405-9053-2 (pob) -- ISBN 978-1-4405-
9054-2 (ebook) -- ISBN 1-4405-9054-0 (ebook)
    1. Unicorns. I. Title.
    GR830.U6A44 2015
    398.24'54--dc23

                    2015012536

Cover design by Erin Dawson.
Cover images © Shutterstock/Gorbash Varvara and Clipart.com.
Interior credits: Clipart.com; Wikimedia Commons; iStockphoto.com/Cattallina/
ttatty/kozzzlova/CoreyFord/Andrew_Howe/ZU_09/JozefKlopacka/ AnnaSuchkova/
Ferdiperdozniy; and Svetlana Alyuk/Sergey Prygov/ ateliersommerland/Gennady
Poddubny/kuco/dazdraperma/Leonard Zhukovsky/123RF.

This book is available at quantity discounts for bulk purchases.
For information, please call 1-800-289-0963.

Dedication

In memory of my wild, strong, and magnificent unicorn,
Ron Conroy—may you be forever free

Always be yourself.
...u can be a
...icorn.
...hat case,
always be a unicorn."

—Elle Lothlorien, *Alice in Wonderland, A Novel*

Acknowledgments

Many thanks to editors Christine Dore, Tom Hardej, Kathryn J. Fallon, and Peter Archer, and the rest of the great staff at Adams Media for making this book a reality.

CONTENTS

The Magic and Mystery of the Unicorn

"Of all the legendary animals of art, folklore and literature, the Unicorn is the one with the greatest hold on our imaginations."

—Nancy Hathaway, *The Unicorn*

STRONG YET GENTLE, innocent yet wise, beautiful beyond imagination, unicorns have fascinated us since the dawn of time. Prehistoric artists painted them on cave walls 15,000 years ago. Alexander the Great claimed to have ridden one. England's Queen Elizabeth I owned two of their horns, worth about $20 million in today's money.

The story of the unicorn is rooted deep in our hearts today, just as our ancestors venerated these magical creatures. The insights that myths, legends, and lore convey resonate with us as *truth*—which is why the unicorn's story has endured for millennia and shows no signs of disappearing. As you flip through the pages of this book, you'll read about what unicorns represent to us, in stories from the ancient past and today.

"The legs, so delicately shaped, balanced a body wrought of finest ivory. And as he moved, his coat shone like reflected moonlight. High on his forehead rose the magic horn, the sign of his uniqueness: a tower held upright by his alert, yet gentle, timid gait."

—Rainer Maria Rilke

Unicorns represent peace and harmony and a compassionate way of living. They teach us that those who possess true power, self-confidence, and wisdom tread gently in the world and care for the innocent and vulnerable. If necessary, unicorns will defend themselves and their kind, but they never do so unless they're attacked first.

Nor do unicorns stoop to lies, chicanery, or stupidity. Instead, they possess the traits of all great heroes: honesty, devotion, respect, inner strength, wisdom, and courage. They can't be bought or manipulated. What's more, they go about their business with genuine modesty, even though they know that they are the most exquisite creatures ever to set foot on Planet Earth. In short, they give us hope. If we let them, they'll guide us toward a more enlightened existence. What's *not* to love?

"My guess is that we seek them not merely for their beauty, even though they are more than beautiful enough. I think they call to our hearts so strongly because they represent something sadly lost; their very presence sings of the ancient wonder pervading the natural world, a sense of wonder hard to hold in these modern times," explains Bruce Coville, author of *A Glory of Unicorns* and The Unicorn Chronicles. "Underlying our desire for unicorns, I suspect, is a longing for purity, a memory of magic, an aching need to recover innocence. In their horns, their eyes, their very being, they carry the hope of healing, the promise of grace."

MEETING THE ELUSIVE UNICORN

e've always admired unicorns' power and majesty. These awe-inspiring creatures might lay their heads in the laps of young ladies and allow children to pat them, yet they retain their properties of strength, intelligence, intuition, and independence. No human can trap a unicorn unless the beast allows it to happen. Its wildness and freedom are part of what entices us; we may be just a bit envious of the unicorn's ability to exist beyond the limitations of our humdrum, everyday world.

Only a virgin can enchant the unicorn. Medieval troubadours, Renaissance painters, and modern-day novelists incorporated this theme into art and literature. The unicorn itself came to symbolize purity on every level. Christianity even chose the unicorn as a symbol for Christ and the virgin as his mother, Mary.

Until the eighteenth century, explorers, adventurers, naturalists, and anthropologists searched the vast plains of Africa, scaled the mountain peaks in Asia, and penetrated deep into the dark forests of Europe in hopes of finding the unicorn. Everywhere they went, they met people who claimed to have seen unicorns—and even hunted them. In this book, you'll read the stories of people who've been fortunate enough to encounter these most magical and mystical of animals.

What Do You Know about Unicorns?

Before we start, let's see how much you already know about unicorns:

- What color are unicorns?
- What animal does the unicorn most closely resemble?
- What is the unicorn's natural enemy?
- What country uses the unicorn as its symbol?
- What creature's horn was often mistaken for the unicorn's?

Of all the strange beasts that have inhabited our world, unicorns are among the most mystical and magical. Their powers can bring blessings to your life, whether you encounter one in person, in a tale told 'round a fire, or in the pages of a book. Let your unicorn quest begin!

PART I

U IS FOR UNICORN

"Now I will believe
That there are unicorns ..."

—William Shakespeare, *The Tempest*

CHAPTER 1

The Unicorn Myth

"Unicorns are immortal. It is their nature to live alone in one place: usually a forest where there is a pool clear enough for them to see themselves—for they are a little vain, knowing themselves to be the most beautiful creatures in all the world, and magic besides."

—Peter S. Beagle, *The Last Unicorn*

SINCE ANTIQUITY, UNICORNS have pranced through the imaginations of people of all ages, in all cultures around the globe. They've inspired some of the world's greatest writers and artists, and intrigued leading figures in history, including Alexander the Great, Julius Caesar, Genghis Khan, Queen Elizabeth I, Marco Polo, and more. Alexander even claimed to have ridden one. But our fascination with the unicorn isn't a thing of the distant past. In fact, the unicorn's popularity is greater now than ever before. A Google search of unicorns turns up more than 60 million results. Amazon lists nearly 15,000 books about unicorns. Dozens of movies and TV shows have featured this magical beast and still captivate audiences today.

Why does this mythical creature continue to beguile us? Obviously, something much deeper and more profound than what initially meets the eye is going on here.

THE STORY OF THE UNICORN

nce upon a time, long, long ago in a land far away, a king and his young daughter lived in a magnificent castle deep within the forest. The princess was the most beautiful human being on earth, kind, innocent, and pure of heart. One sunny day, the girl decided to go for a walk in the woods to collect wildflowers. All around her, she heard the songs of birds and delighted in the rainbow colors of the flowers at her feet.

But as she wandered deeper into the forest, the birdsong ceased and the flowers vanished. Now the frightened princess saw only tangled vines, gnarled trees, and parched grass, and she realized she'd become hopelessly lost. As the sun set in the west, the vines began tugging at the girl's gown, dragging her farther into the dark woods, and she fainted from fear.

When she awoke, the princess found herself lying in a clearing. Nearby, she spotted a delicate creature as beautiful as herself. It resembled a small, white horse or perhaps a deer, but with a single, spiral-shaped horn sprouting from its forehead. She wondered in amazement—*could it be?*

For centuries people had told tales of the mythical unicorn, an animal of such grace, perfection, and virtue that none could compare to it. But its most incredible quality was its magical horn, which everyone believed would cure illness and purify poisoned water. In an attempt to obtain that wondrous horn, men had hunted the gentle unicorn for many years but none had ever captured it.

The radiant white beast trotted toward the princess, recognizing in her another soul as pure as itself, and knelt beside her. No longer afraid, the princess climbed on the unicorn's back and they galloped through the dark forest back to the castle.

But when they arrived at the palace and the king's men laid eyes on the unicorn, the soldiers grabbed their spears and sharpened their swords. *At last,* they thought, *we shall ensnare the wondrous creature and take its magical horn*—and they quickly surrounded it.

"No, no!" cried the princess, wrapping her arms around the unicorn's neck.

Then the king emerged from the palace and approached his daughter, but the girl refused to let go of the unicorn. "Father, you must protect him. He rescued me when I became lost in the forest. He saved my life."

The king ordered his men to sheath their weapons and waved them all away. He hugged the princess and thanked the unicorn for bringing her home safe. As he gazed into the beast's lovely blue eyes, the king realized that of all the world's creatures, the unicorn was the purest and most innocent. Thus, he proclaimed the unicorn to be a sacred animal and forbade anyone ever to hunt it. The king opened the castle's gates and freed the unicorn—and no one except the pure of heart would ever see it again.

CHRISTIANITY AND THE UNICORN

During the first centuries of Christianity, as the new religion gained ground in the Middle East and Europe, the story of the unicorn became interwoven with the story of Christ. Early Christians created an allegory that associated the unicorn with Jesus because of its purity, whereas the maiden princess represented the Virgin Mary. The unicorn's magical horn, with its power to dissolve poison, served as a metaphor for Christ the Redeemer removing sin from the world. The hunt for the unicorn symbolized the Passion of Christ. Later, during the medieval and Renaissance periods, this version of the myth inspired great tapestries, mosaics, and other religious artwork (see Chapters 5 and 6).

According to another story, the unicorn appeared in the Garden of Eden. Adam, having been given the honor of naming the animals, chose to name the exquisitely beautiful unicorn first. Some tales say that when Adam and Eve were banished from the Garden, only the loyal unicorn came away with them. According to Saint Hildegard von Bingen (1098–1179), however, the innocent unicorn was allowed to return to Paradise once every century. While there, it drank the sacred waters and ate the holy vegetation that grew only in that heavenly realm, and thus renewed its strength.

The Garden of Eden by Lucas Cranach the Elder, 1530

Unicorns in the Bible

The unicorn turns up in the Bible in a number of places. In the King James Version of the *Book of Daniel* 8:5, for instance, Daniel has a vision of a strange animal: "And as I was considering, behold, a he-goat came from the west on the face of the whole earth, and touched not the ground: and the goat had a notable horn between his eyes."

Other references include:

- "God brought them out of Egypt; he hath as it were the strength of an unicorn." (Numbers 23:22)
- "His glory is like the firstling of his bullock, and his horns are like the horns of unicorns: with them he shall push the people together to the ends of the earth." (Deuteronomy 33:17)
- "Save me from the lion's mouth; for thou hast heard me from the horns of unicorns." (Psalms 22:21)
- "He maketh them [the cedars of Lebanon] also to skip like a calf; Lebanon and Sirion like a young unicorn." (Psalms 29:6)
- "But my horn shalt thou exalt like the horn of the unicorn: I shall be anointed with fresh oil." (Psalms 92:10)
- "And the unicorns shall come down with them, and the bullocks with their bulls; and their land shall be soaked with blood, and their dust made fat with fatness." (Isaiah 34:7)

However, not all texts consider the animal mentioned in the Old Testament to be a unicorn. The Babylonian Talmud, for one, calls it a *tachash*, an ancient multicolored desert animal with a single horn. After helping to build the Tabernacle, mythology tells us the *tachash* became extinct.

The *Re'em*

The unicorn's inclusion in the Bible dates back to the period between 300 and 200 B.C.E., when a group of seventy scholars in Alexandria, Egypt, embarked on the task of translating ancient Jewish scripture into Greek. Among these texts they found the word *re'em*, which in Hebrew referred to a large, horned beast. The scholars translated the word as *monokeros*, meaning "one horn." Most likely, these interpreters had knowledge of the earlier unicorn legends that had existed for centuries before the time of Christ. Like the unicorn, the wild *re'em* was notoriously untamable as well as strong and graceful, so their take on it is understandable.

They produced a work known as the *Septuagint*, which served as an early source for the Old Testament of the Bible. The translators of the 1611 Authorized King James Version picked up this interpretation and repeated it—and so the unicorn continued to grace the pages of Christianity's holy book for centuries.

No Unicorns on Noah's Ark

A legend claims that the reason unicorns no longer exist on earth is that, when it came time for all the animals to get on Noah's Ark, these independent creatures refused. Instead, they continued frolicking with their fellows as the Ark weighed anchor. Another tale says that Noah decided he couldn't take both the lions and the unicorns on the boat because these longtime enemies would just end up fighting the whole time. He chose to save the lions instead of the unicorns.

According to Geraldine McCaughrean in her 1997 children's book *Unicorns! Unicorns!* the compassionate unicorns missed the boat because they helped the other animals get onboard, instead of trying to save themselves. Shel Silverstein, in his poem "The Unicorn" from the poetry collection *Where the Sidewalk Ends*, tells us the unicorns hid from Noah, "playin' silly games" as the rain began pelting down, and thus got left behind. Silverstein's lyrics were later put to music in a popular song by the Irish Rovers.

Some versions of this story say the unicorns swam beside the Ark for forty days and forty nights, but never came onboard. As a result, the unicorn became extinct after the Flood.

"The Giant of the Flood" in *Jewish Fairy Tales and Legends*, by Aunt Naomi (1919), however, tells us that the unicorn did, in fact, survive the Flood. In her version of the tale, Noah wants to save the unicorn from the deluge he realizes is imminent, but he doesn't know where to find one. A giant named Og, who hopes Noah will save him too, fetches the sought-after unicorn—but the beast is so enormous that it won't fit on the Ark. Instead, Noah decides to tie it by its horn to the Ark so the unicorn can swim alongside. Og climbs onto the creature's back and rides along as well for forty days and forty nights, until the waters recede and the Ark comes to rest atop Mount Ararat. From then on, the giant becomes Noah's servant.

Aunt Naomi's story doesn't explain how the unicorn perpetuated itself through the ages, however, considering that only one of its species came along for the big boat ride. Perhaps unicorns, being the magical creatures we know them to be, can clone themselves or reproduce asexually, like algae. Hey, it could happen, right?

SYMBOLS OF COURTLY LOVE

uring the late medieval period, around the end of the eleventh century or so, ideas about love and relationships between men and women started to change—at least among members of the court. Beginning in the south of France, poets and troubadours touted the concept of *amour courtois* or courtly love, which soon spread to other parts of Europe and Britain. This highly structured, formalized code of behavior stated that a male suitor must worship and serve his lady—a woman who, by the way, was usually *not* his wife.

The Five Features of Courtly Love

According to Irving Singer, author of *The Nature of Love*, courtly love consisted of five features:

"(1) Sexual love between men and women is *in itself* something splendid, an ideal worth striving for; (2) love ennobles both the lover and the beloved; (3) being an ethical and aesthetic attainment, sexual love cannot be reduced to mere libidinal impulse; (4) love pertains to courtesy and courtship but is not necessarily related to the institution of marriage; (5) love is an intense, passionate relationship that establishes a holy oneness between man and woman."

At the time, marriages among the royalty and nobility were arranged for political reasons, and love rarely factored into these matches. Therefore, a man's passion and erotic love were diverted to another source: a lady of the court whom he promised to honor, obey, and pledge himself—even to the point of death. Such idealized romances, however, weren't supposed to be consummated, as the church considered infidelity a mortal sin.

Chivalry and thwarted desire fueled much great literature and art of the period. Soon, poets, musicians, and artists began linking the courtly lover with the unicorn and his lady with the virgin to whom the beast is drawn. The unicorn myth had always contained spiritual elements and the ideal of chaste devotion, so the symbolism seemed a natural extension: a wild and powerful creature who can be tamed only by a virtuous maiden.

"That the maiden and the Unicorn are more like chaste and secret lovers—And that a virgin ignorant of corporeal desire is more likely to receive wisdoms of the spirit."

—Michael Green, *De Historia et Veritate Unicornis*

A Symbol of Chivalry

"Considering that chastity was one of the foremost chivalric virtues, we are not surprised to find the unicorn figured on many knightly seals and coats of arms," writes Odell Shepard in *The Lore of the Unicorn.* "There was something essentially aristocratic about him. His kinship to the horse, always associated with knighthood, was suggestive, but more important was the headlong enthusiasm of his devotion to beautiful women. He was fierce and proud and dangerous to his foes, as a knight should be, and he was also gentle; he had the dignity of solitude; he was beautiful and strong; most significant of all, he was a protector and champion of other beasts against the wiles of their enemies."

ASIAN UNICORNS

hus far we've talked mostly about unicorns in the Western tradition, but Asia and the Middle East also have rich bodies of unicorn folklore. Eastern mythology tells us that the unicorn was the first created and the most perfect of all animals ever to inhabit earth. So compassionate was this beautiful creature that it wouldn't hurt a fly—literally. In fact, it delicately avoided crushing insects when it walked and wouldn't even eat fruit; its hooves barely skimmed the grass. Perhaps this reflects the concept of *ahimsa* in Hindu, Buddhist, and Jain doctrines, which honors the sacredness in all beings and prohibits anyone from inflicting injury on any creature.

The gentle and wild unicorn, legend said, would continue to shun the world and stay hidden in the mystical realms until human beings gave up their evil ways. Only then would the unicorn allow itself to be tamed, for then neither it nor any animal on earth would suffer fear or pain again.

"It was said to be so sensitive it could feel the weight of a shadow cast by the light of the moon. All animals became tame around the unicorn. Rain and fire did its bidding, and when it plucked a leaf, two grew in its place. The unicorn's voice was sweet and delicate, with the sound of a thousand wind chimes."

—All about Unicorns, *www.allaboutunicorns.com*

The Chinese Qilin

Chinese mythology speaks of a fanciful and auspicious creature called the *qilin*. This hybrid beast often combines the body of a deer or a tiger, the tail of an ox, the hooves of a horse, and the head of a dragon. Not only that, it also sports the green scales of a fish. Some depictions show it with wings, or at least give it the ability to fly, signified by clouds at its feet. A single horn protrudes from its forehead, but it sometimes curves backward, unlike the typical Western unicorn's straight, spiral-shaped horn.

Considered one of the "Four Benevolent Animals," the qilin was said to rule over all the other terrestrial creatures. As such, it offered protection, guidance, and prosperity to those who respected it. It also possessed the gift of prophesy. And, like its Western cousin, the qilin was linked with purity, harmony, and gentleness.

Other sources, including *Chinese Mythology* by Anthony Christie, describe the qilin (*k'i-lin* or *chii-lin*) as having the body of a deer, the tail and hooves of an ox, and the requisite single horn. This Chinese unicorn is portrayed as intelligent and just, a being

that supports goodness and never harms anyone except those who are evil. It only appeared to wise rulers. When a qilin was sighted, it confirmed that the emperor had heaven's blessing and the legitimate right to rule his people.

Military Unicorns

During the Qing dynasty in China, which lasted from 1644 until 1911, the qilin became a symbol of first-grade military officials of the Imperial Court. Believed to possess intelligence and the power to bring a family prosperity and success, the mystical creature also represented high moral character.

Japan's Kirin

In Japanese mythology we find the *kirin* and the *sin-you*. The kirin displays the shy, docile nature we usually associate with unicorns in the West, but the sin-you has a more judgmental side. Legend says it possessed the ability to determine right from wrong and could see into the souls of people to perceive their guilt or innocence. If the sin-you decided someone was guilty, it sentenced the wrongdoer to death and impaled the culprit through the heart with its horn.

The Drink of Unicorns

What do unicorns drink? How about Kirin Ichiban beer? Since its introduction in 1998, Kirin Ichiban has made its mark among beer lovers in both the East and the West. The unicorn's auspicious symbolism, plus its connection with peace and prosperity, were good reasons to name a tasty brew after him. Kirin Ichiban's manufacturers capitalized on the unicorn's legendary purity when naming their product and use the slogan "Beer at Its Purest." If you don't speak Japanese, *ichiban* means "first."

Vietnamese and Korean Unicorns

Vietnamese folklore mentions a creature called the *qué ly* or *lan* that bears similarities to the unicorn. It first made an appearance about 2,700 years ago in tales from the Duong Dynasty, where it symbolized prosperity. Like the Chinese, the Vietnamese consider the unicorn to be one of the four sacred creatures—along with the dragon, the phoenix, and the tortoise—and have decorated many temples with its image.

Westerners might have a hard time identifying the qué ly or qué lan as a unicorn, however, for it usually appears with a dragon-like head and the body of a horse. Some descriptions say it has the mouth of a crocodile, the nose of a lion, the ears of a dog, and the feet and horn of a deer. It may even have fish scales covering its body and a moustache like a catfish's. Furthermore, it can change its appearance, so it won't look the same at all times to all people. A benevolent creature, the Vietnamese unicorn is believed to bring good luck, happiness, and longevity.

Heralds of the Rains

The Vietnamese celebrate the unicorn on the full moon of the eighth month by dressing up in costumes and masks. The festivities include hanging an effigy of a unicorn and shooting arrows at it while people sing. Tradition says that after the celebration is finished and the singing stops, the annual monsoon rains will begin.

In 2011, the Korean Central News Agency circulated a news report speculating that the *Kiringul*, translated as the "Unicorn Lair," had been located in North Korea, thus claiming Kiringul. However, Kiringul's historical significance also spills over into

mythology as an ancient site visited by King Tongmyong, the founder of the ancient kingdom of Koguryo, who supposedly rode a kirin. Neither remains nor living kirins were discovered at the lair.

The Persian Karkadann

Persian culture has its version of the unicorn, too, but unlike the gentle creatures of Western mythology, their *karkadann* comes across as a ferocious warrior. Persian legends describe it as having three hooves on each leg, which make it seem as if the beast would lumber about clumsily tripping over its own feet, rather than displaying the grace we usually associate with unicorns. Some tales say it has six eyes and nine mouths, but can change its shape at will. Most impressive is the creature's horn of pure gold. Said to be born in the midst of battle, this fierce animal resembles a rhinoceros with a lion's tail. Perhaps the rhino did, indeed, foster the conception of the karkadann in the minds of its believers, for its prominent horn curves like that of the rhinoceros.

Whereas Western myths almost universally laud the unicorn as a peace-loving entity, its Middle Eastern counterpart is said to have exhibited a more aggressive nature and intimidated all the other animals, who gave it a wide berth—all except the ring dove. Folklore says the karkadann had a particular fascination with the bird's song and languished beneath trees where the dove lived, waiting for it to light on the huge beast's horn.

Other lore from the Middle East presents a kinder, gentler vision of the karkadann. Described as having physical characteristics similar to those of a stag, horse, or antelope, this herbivore tended to be mild-mannered—until it encountered its deadly enemy, the elephant. Like the unicorn in Western folklore, this Middle Eastern unicorn could purify water simply by immersing its horn in a stream, pond, or lake—but with one additional result: when it did, all the females in the vicinity immediately became pregnant.

Unicorns in India

Sometime around 400 B.C.E., the Greek historian Ctesias stated that the unicorn lived in India—and he's not the only one who claimed that (see Chapter 4). Legends and literature say a one-horned animal much like an antelope called a *ŕśya* in Sanskrit abides in the region, or at least did in the past. The ancient Sanskrit epic the *Mahābhārata* even mentions a mythological humanlike being named Ŕśyaśrnga who had a horn in his forehead.

According to Dr. Gautama V. Vajracharya, scholar and art historian at the University of Wisconsin–Madison, ancient carved seals from the Indus Valley show a very specific animal with a single, S-shaped, ribbed horn. He points out that this image is not at all like those of deer, bulls, water buffalo, or other animals also engraved on similar seals. Three-dimensional sculptures of the rśya also show it with just one horn. This doesn't necessarily mean such an animal existed physically, however, for Indian artists were also fond of portraying mythic creatures, such as many-headed beasts and tigers with horns.

Nancy Hathaway, in her book *The Unicorn*, relates a story of a man in India named Vibhandaka who marries a unicorn. One day after the death of a holy sage who had been his beloved teacher for years, the grieving young man sits meditating in a cave. A beautiful creature, similar to a gazelle but with only one horn instead of two, approaches the lonely Vibhandaka. The young man falls in love with the gentle unicorn and the two marry. In time, they have a son whom they name Rishyashringa, who looks pretty much like an ordinary human except for one peculiar detail: a horn protruding from the center of his forehead.

A SYMBOL OF "COMING OF AGE"

et's take another look at the unicorn story summarized at the beginning of this chapter. From a psychological perspective, this legend could be interpreted another way: as a coming-of-age story. Here we have a beautiful, kind, and innocent young maiden who ventures into the forest to pick flowers. She leaves the safety of her father's castle, which signifies childhood, to explore unfamiliar territory by herself. The forest has long represented mystery, the unknown, and the dark side of human nature—which modern psychology interprets as the subconscious/unconscious or the "shadow." Flowers, of course, are the most overtly sexual of all earth's inhabitants, unabashedly flaunting their reproductive organs for all to see.

Not surprisingly, the innocent maiden gets lost in the convoluted forest, which symbolizes the tangle of emotions and desires that draw an unsuspecting young girl into the confusing realm of womanhood. Now she's awash in the confluence of mysteries and secrets she's been warned against, and she's scared. So scared, she swoons.

When the princess awakens, she eyes her redeemer nearby: the perfect, pure, and powerful unicorn—instantly identifiable by his huge horn. If you've ever looked into Freudian psychology, you'll quickly make the connection: the unicorn's horn is an obvious phallic symbol. The helpless virgin is now in the presence of a great, immortal, and obviously male sage who will teach her the ancient mysteries of love and sex, and initiate her into the next stage of her female life.

But unlike the crude, rash, bloodthirsty soldiers in her father's command, the unicorn embodies gentleness and wisdom. He lays his head lovingly in her lap, then rescues her from the frightening forest—freeing her from her fears and showing her the sensual pleasures available to her, now that she's transitioned from childhood into maturity.

The princess stands firm against her father's soldiers. In doing so, she represents the power of love and its triumph over cruelty, symbolized by the king's army. At the story's conclusion, the princess demands that her father's army release the unicorn—an indication, perhaps, of a woman accepting her own strength, her ability to make her own decisions, and to stand up for her beliefs in the face of adversity.

So, is the myth of the unicorn a fanciful story that might grace the "Romance" section in your local bookstore? Or one that bespeaks a feminist philosophy? Maybe a little of both. It might also praise the joyous union of male and female in a sacred sense. Like all enduring myths, the tale of the lady and the unicorn transcends a simple storyline and reveals fundamental truths that abide deep within us.

As Bruce Coville writes in his book, *Into the Land of Unicorns,* "Wherever they may have come from, and wherever they may have gone, unicorns live inside the true believer's heart. Which means as long as we can dream, there will be unicorns."

CHAPTER 2

The Origins of the Unicorn

*"In the heart of the forest a unicorn is born.
The trees hold gentle branches around it, the forest
pools guard its secret; only the stars can see.
Among the silent spaces of the trees it grows
protected, nurtured."*

—Josephine Bradley, *In Pursuit of the Unicorn*

THE PEOPLE OF EARTH have believed in magic since the dawn of time. Magic infused their daily lives and enriched their existence in countless ways. But one day, the fairies noticed that humans were beginning to lose interest in magic and were turning their attention toward more pragmatic concerns. Knowing that the world would cease to exist if the magic died, the fairies chose the most exquisite and enchanting creature in the universe and sent it to earth, so that all who looked upon it would fall under its spell and instantly rekindle their faith. So goes one myth of how the unicorn came to abide in the world among us.

Another creation tale, recounted in *De Historia et Veritate Unicornis*, says that the unicorn descended to earth on a cloud. The first-born creature, he was called Asallam. His role was that of the light-bearer and guide, the one who would drive away darkness from the face of the earth, for his horn itself was a beacon formed of spiraling light. With that laser-like horn he speared a rock and brought forth life-giving water to produce the most magnificent garden ever known. Soon after, the Holy One breathed man into the garden. The unicorn was the first animal the man beheld. At first sight, the unicorn loved the man and knelt before him—and from that day forth, Fate has bound the two beings together for eternity.

Despite these and other legends about the genesis of unicorns, we can't help wondering where these beautiful beasts really came from. Why has such a large body of mythology and folklore evolved around them? What inspired the idea of these mysterious creatures in the first place? Does a physical precedent exist? Is it possible that unicorns really trod this earth once upon a time, and might they one day return? Let's explore these ideas further.

A Travel Guide to the Realm of Mythic Beasts

Said to be the first illustrated travel guide ever printed, the *Peregrinatio in Terram Sanctam* published in 1486 introduced European readers to the wonders that existed beyond their own circumscribed world. Based on a pilgrimage to Jerusalem and Egypt, the book contained a number of woodcuts done by one of the travelers, Erhard Reuwich. Many of the artist's illustrations depicted cities he viewed during his sojourn—but he also included images of strange animals he observed, among them camels, crocodiles, and a unicorn.

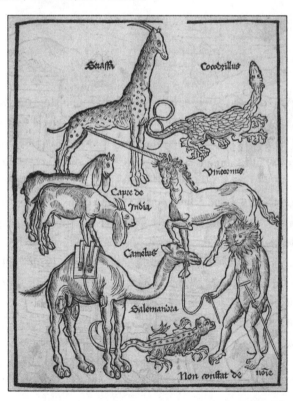

"Its origins are lost in the mists of the mythical Source: some legends suggest it came from Tibet, others speak of India, still others point to the Mountains of the Moon in Africa. New Age thinkers are convinced the unicorn originated in Atlantis."

—Symbol Reader, *www.symbolreader.net*

GOATS AND BULLS

ncient rock carvings and cave paintings show evidence of unicorns and may explain where they came from. Archaeologists have discovered millennia-old images of bulls and goats in Europe, Egypt and the Middle East, and parts of Asia. In some of our world's earliest cultures, deities and mythological beings were pictured as animals or animal amalgams, sometimes with horns. For example, the Egyptian goddess Hathor often wears a headpiece adorned with cow's horns that represent fertility and motherhood. In the Mithraic faith, the Roman god Mithras was linked with the bull. The Celtic mythical figure Cernunnos sports the antlers of a wild stag on the top of his head.

But all these animals have two horns—unless you view them in profile. Then the two horns appear as one. Many early murals, in fact, depict goats and bulls from the side, which makes it seem as if the animals have only a single horn jutting from the center of their foreheads, just like a unicorn. Furthermore, goats and cattle have cloven hooves, and goats have beards—features shared by many early unicorns. Might our ancestors have based their idea of unicorns on these commonplace animals?

Unicorns in Pakistan

More than 4,500 years ago, people living in the vicinity of Harappa (now in Pakistan) in the Indus Valley engraved stones with pictures of animals. Archaeologists believe these carved stones were used as the seals or insignia of important people. One of the animals depicted on these seals resembles our modern-day conceptions of a unicorn. However, researchers think that the "unicorn" was probably an aurochs, a type of wild bull, and that because the images appear in profile, it looks as if the beast only has one horn.

THE RHINOCEROS

nother theory suggests that the rhinoceros may have given rise to stories of the unicorn. Fifty thousand years ago, a now extinct animal called the *Elasmotherium* roamed Eurasia. By some accounts, it bore a slight resemblance to a very large horse. This huge, hairy beast had a single, long, pointed horn on its forehead. In the late nineteenth century, the magazine *Nature* reported on a version of this animal, described by researcher Alexander Brandt, and the Russian journal *Niwa* published an illustration of the beast. Brandt had heard about unicorns from the legends of the Siberian Tatars. Could there be a link between the two?

Rhinoceros—including a white rhino—also existed in Southeast Asia and Africa in those days. Rhinos once inhabited regions of South America, too. These creatures coexisted with

humans during the time ancient artists immortalized the unicorn in cave art—might they have inspired our ancestors' visions?

The natives of Chiloé, Chile, speak of a blue-green unicorn about the size of a year-old calf, with a single silver horn protruding from its head. Also known as a "sea horse," this rhino-like beast is reputed to have sharp teeth and claws and is said to feed not only on fish, but also on human beings. The fanciful creature may have been based on the elephant seal.

UNICORN SIGHTINGS

During his travels in Asia during the late thirteenth century, the Venetian merchant and explorer, Marco Polo, claimed to have sighted a unicorn. According to his account, "There are wild elephants and plenty of unicorns, which are scarcely smaller than elephants. They have the hair of a buffalo and feet like an elephant's. They have a single large black horn in the middle of the forehead . . . They have a head like a wild boar's and always carry it stooped toward the ground. They spend their time by preference wallowing in mud and slime. They are very ugly brutes to look at. They are not at all such as we describe them when we relate that they let themselves be captured by virgins." Clearly, the Italian adventurer had spotted a rhino, not a unicorn.

When the horned skull of an Ice Age rhino was discovered in Austria in the fourteenth century, people first believed it had come from a dragon, not a unicorn. The fossilized skull served as a model for a sculpture, which now stands in the town of Klagenfurt. You can still see the skull in the town's Naturhistorisches Landesmuseum.

DEER AND ANTELOPE

ne of the most plausible theories of where our conceptions of unicorns originated suggests that various species of deer and/or antelope served as the prototypes for unicorn legends. Like images of goats and bulls, many early drawings of these animals show them from the side, so that only one of their two horns can be seen.

The Oryx

This type of antelope, native to Africa and the Arabian Peninsula, might have been mistaken for a unicorn. However, its long, thin horns slope backward from its forehead rather than forward, as is the case in most portrayals of unicorns.

The Eland

Ancient petroglyphs in southern Africa depict another type of plains antelope, larger than the oryx, called an eland. The indigenous people of this region gave the animal spiritual significance in their rituals and used its fat to concoct medicinal remedies. Like the oryx, the eland's long, thin horns slope back from its forehead, though, instead of forward. The 1,500-pound eland's ability to kill lions that prey on its herds may have spawned the long-standing legends of animosity between Africa's large cats and unicorns, and of unicorns using their horns to defend themselves against lions (see Chapter 6).

The Blackbuck Antelope

Native to Pakistan and India, the blackbuck is a smaller antelope than the eland—adult males weigh in at about 100–150 pounds. Its long, pointed, corkscrew-shaped horns more closely resemble the unicorn's (and the narwhal's) than those of the eland, oryx, and other members of the deer or antelope families. The white horns project from the male antelope's forehead in much the same manner as the unicorn's (except, of course, the antelope has two rather than one) and can extend up to more than thirty inches in length. Adult males are black on their backs and white on their stomachs and legs (young bucks are tan and white)—but, of course, our conception of the pure white unicorn didn't come about until the medieval period. Shy and amazingly swift, these graceful creatures can race across even rocky terrain at high speeds and they seem to fly when they jump. If a deer-like creature served as the model for a unicorn, the blackbuck comes closest to fitting the bill.

The Roe Deer

A small, woodland creature native to the British Isles and Europe, the delicate roe deer features slender, pointed antlers shorter than those of the oryx, blackbuck, or eland. In 2008, a roe deer with a single antler in the center of its forehead was discovered in Italy. Although it's not unusual to see deer with only one antler—the second one having been broken off in a fight or accident—the remaining single antler usually protrudes from one side of the deer's head instead of the middle. This Italian curiosity may have resulted from a genetic abnormality.

In 2014, *National Geographic* reported the story of a similar roe deer, shot by a hunter in Slovenia. Scientists speculated that the deer might have been injured in its youth, and the trauma caused its antlers to fuse rather than growing normally.

The Emperor's Unicorns

The Chinese unicorn, known as the qilin, became confused with the giraffe in the fifteenth century, when the Chinese ship captain and general Zheng He brought back a pair of these giant beasts from Africa as a gift for the emperor. The fuzzy, horn-like ossicones on the giraffes' foreheads caused those who saw them to believe the long-necked animals were unicorns.

FABRICATED "UNICORNS"

Can you fabricate a unicorn? In the 1930s, Dr. W. Franklin Dove, a biologist at the University of Maine, decided to give it a try. Horns, he knew, didn't actually grow out of an animal's skull—instead, they started out as tissue that later fused with the bone. Consequently, he reasoned it would be possible to modify the natural growth pattern of the horns. Dr. Dove selected a day-old calf for his experiment. He removed the calf's two horn buds, reshaped them so they'd grow together, and implanted the altered buds back into the middle of the calf's forehead. The experiment worked. The calf grew only one horn, about a foot long.

The young bull's single spike proved stronger and more effective than the normal two separated horns when it came to fighting. But oddly enough, the unibull lacked the aggressiveness often associated with his fellows and displayed a gentler nature, like that of a unicorn. Did the animal's confidence in his superior skill mean he didn't need to strut his stuff?

Dr. Dove wrote a paper describing his study called "The Physiology of Horn Growth" and the *Journal of Experimental Zoology* published it in 1935. The following year, *Scientific Monthly* published another of Dr. Dove's articles, "Artificial Production of the Fabulous Unicorn."

Half a century later, unicorns began appearing in sideshows around the United States and they even traveled with the Ringling Bros. and Barnum & Bailey Circus. As it turned out, however, the beasts were actually surgically modified goats whose horns had been merged using Dr. Dove's technique.

On the Spring Equinox in 1980, Oberon Zell-Ravenheart and his wife Morning Glory, produced their first "unicorn" using Dr. Dove's methodology. They named it Lancelot. Oberon wrote affectionately of their unusual pet, on New Page Books's blogsite in June 2011: "His white coat was iridescent in sunlight, with the texture of satin, and his long mane was like cloud fluff." From their research, the couple deduced that unicorns may have existed on earth as various species, which evolved over time, as all species do. "Such an animal would, in effect, be fundamentally different from its ancestral stock, elevated so profoundly that it would develop as a different animal."

Horns and Antlers

What's the difference between horns and antlers? Horns, such as those found on antelope, goats, sheep, and cattle, are composed of a core made of bone and a cover of keratin—the same material that comprises your hair and fingernails. A deer's antlers start out as cartilage and turn to bone, growing from the animal's forehead as an extension of its skull. Horns continue to grow throughout the animal's lifetime, but if they get broken they won't grow back. Deer, on the other hand, shed their antlers and grow new ones again each year.

THE NARWHAL

nter the narwhal, sometimes called the "unicorn of the sea." This small, elusive whale that swims in the Arctic waters bears no resemblance to a unicorn—except for its amazing "horn." One of the male narwhal's teeth grows through his upper lip and looks like a spike on its head; this spike can grow more than ten feet long and spirals in a counterclockwise direction. Researchers also think that the tusk might give the whale the ability to sense changes in water temperature and pressure.

According to the American Museum of Natural History's website *www.amnh.org*, the narwhal's long, white, spiral-shaped tusk set the standard for a unicorn's horn. Before the Vikings and Danish sailors introduced the tusk into the rest of Europe—passing it off as a unicorn's horn and garnering huge profits—legends described unicorns as having horns of various shapes, sizes, and colors. Once the exquisite, pure-white narwhal's tusk made its appearance, it became the *sine qua non* of the mystical unicorn's horn—with astounding results.

The Unicorn Throne

The Throne of Denmark in Copenhagen has a magical secret: It's made of unicorn horns—or so the story goes. Built in the seventeenth century, the opulent ivory and gold chair that serves as the physical seat of the country's monarchy was inspired by the biblical King Solomon's throne. Three life-sized lion sculptures fashioned of silver guard the throne. But before you unicorn lovers start texting PETA, let it be known that the story is a hoax. No unicorns died in the construction of the Danish throne—it's really fabricated from narwhal tusks.

CHAPTER 3

How to Recognize a Unicorn

"The unicorn was white, with hoofs of silver and graceful horn of pearl . . . The glorious thing about him was his eye. There was a faint bluish furrow down each side of his nose, and this led to the eye sockets, and surrounded them in a pensive shade. The eyes, circled by this sad and beautiful darkness, were so sorrowful, lonely, gentle and nobly tragic, that they killed all other emotions except love."

—T.H. White, *The Once and Future King*

EVERYONE KNOWS WHAT a unicorn looks like, right? It's a horsey sort of animal with a long, curlicue horn that juts out from the center of its forehead. It has a pure-white coat, and an elegant, flowing mane and tail. Of course, today's playful unicorns also come in a rainbow of colors with lots of sparkles, wings à la Pegasus—and occasionally bizarre attributes you probably don't want to think too much about. But that wasn't always the case.

In earlier times, in Western culture, unicorns appeared as hybrid creatures with the torso of a horse or deer, the beard and cloven hooves of a goat, and a lion's tail. Eastern unicorns often feature scales and other dragon-like qualities. Let's take a closer look, now, at this most beloved and mysterious creature to learn more about its characteristics, lifestyle, and environment.

"She did not look anything like a horned horse, as unicorns are often pictured, being small and cloven-hooved, possessing that oldest, wildest grace that horses have never had, that deer only have in a shy, thin imitation and goats in dancing mockery. Her neck was long and slender, making her head seem smaller than it was, and the mane that fell almost to the middle of her back was soft as dandelion fluff and as fine as cirrus. She had pointed ears and thin legs, with feathers of white hair at the ankles; and the long horn above her eyes shone and shivered with its own seashell light even in the deepest midnight."

—Peter S. Beagle, *The Last Unicorn*

THE UNICORN'S HORN

Undoubtedly its most distinctive feature, the unicorn's horn is also its most magical. The spiral shape symbolizes the spiraling pattern of life energy, recognized by metaphysicians from ancient times until the present. Spiritually, the spiral signifies movement from the secret depths of your center outward into the world at large—and back again. It also suggests the soul's movement from earthly existence upward toward the higher levels of consciousness. We see the symbol echoed in Native American petroglyphs, Celtic art, and Zen gardens. Swiss psychiatrist C.G. Jung considered the spiral to be an archetype for the energy force in our cosmos—what yogis refer to as the kundalini—and of course, the Milky Way is spiral-shaped.

> *"A wise man never plays leapfrog with a unicorn."*
>
> —Tibetan proverb

An Instrument of Purification

This most magnificent of all creatures can plunge his long, spiraled horn into poisoned waters and cleanse them, so that all earth's creatures can drink safely and be nourished. His purity is so profound that it affects whatever he touches—no taint or corruption or illness or evil can stand up to the unicorn's righteousness. Like the Christ (with whom Christian mythology links the unicorn), the unicorn's purity neutralizes the poisons that afflict the world.

"The animal is most readily associated with the new or crescent moon, which might indeed seem to dwellers by the sea to be leading the stars down to the water and to dip its own horn therein before they descend."

—Odell Shepard, *The Lore of the Unicorn*

Legends blame a serpent for contaminating the waters—another Christian allegory. Ever since the Garden of Eden, the serpent has gotten a bad rap, so it's no surprise that folklore paints him as the culprit in this story too. Marianna Mayer's book *The Unicorn and the Lake,* lavishly illustrated by Michael Hague, presents the ancient tale to modern-day children. In it, the glorious white unicorn battles with the giant, evil, red serpent and eventually overcomes it, symbolizing Christ's triumph over the devil.

Poison and Treachery in the Middle Ages

It's interesting to note that during the medieval period in Europe, as the unicorn myth was gaining popularity among the aristocracy, so was poisoning as a way to rid oneself of one's enemies. According to Dartmouth University's website, "In Italy, during the Middle Ages, the most widely accused of poisoners were the Borgias, Pope Alexander VI, and his son, Cesare. Most say that Cesare's half-sister, Lucretia, was innocent of the Borgias's involvement in wholesale applied toxicology, but even today her name is irrevocably linked to the surreptitious use of arsenic."

In reaction to the widespread intrigue and murderousness of the times—and the underlying, surreptitious malevolence that persisted among the conflicting powers in Europe—the unicorn arose as a symbol of righteousness, devotion, and honesty, and its horn as an antidote to evil. At a time when wine and water could easily be laced with poison, who wouldn't seek the magic of the unicorn's horn to erase all traces of toxins?

However, even if arsenic or other poisons hadn't been intentionally introduced into a beverage, the waters of medieval Europe were rife with impurities. Typhoid, for example, lurked in the public water supply, and not only commoners but also members of the aristocracy, including England's King John (brother of Richard the Lionheart), died from dysentery that resulted from drinking contaminated water.

It's no surprise, therefore, that the unicorn's purifying horn, which legend said could protect both humans and animals from poisoning, held tremendous appeal. That appeal led the royal classes, and anyone else who could afford to do so, to purchase cups supposedly made of unicorn horn that would safeguard them against the omnipresent threat of poisoning.

The Unicorn's Protective Properties

In her twelfth-century *Physica*, the German abbess Saint Hildegard von Bingen recommended using more than just the unicorn's horn to guard against illness: "From unicorn skin, make a belt. Gird yourself with it against your skin, and no strong disease or fever will harm your insides. Also, make shoes from its skin and wear them. You will always have healthy feet, legs, and loins. No disease will harm you in these places. [A person who fears being killed by poison should put unicorn hoof under the dish where his food is, or under the cup containing his drink. If they are hot and there is poison in them, it will make them boil in the vessel; if they are cold, it will make them smoke, and he will be able to tell there is poison in them.] Other parts of the unicorn are suitable for medicine."

Although the unicorn's horn was considered the most powerful and precious of all purifying substances, medieval and Renaissance people ascribed magical qualities to other materials as well. Serpentine or "snake stone," a dark-green stone with black specks, was also prized for its ability to protect against poisons and was used in making tableware. "The constant fear of poisoning gave rise to strict ceremonial rules for courtly banquets. The cup-bearer or court official precutting the meat touched the food with a piece of unicorn horn (narwhal tusk), viper's tongue (petrified sharks' teeth), or serpentine to ascertain that the food was innocuous," explain the editors of *Princely Splendor: The Dresden Court 1580–1620*.

Red coral, too, had its place on the tables of the nobility, especially in Germany. Believed to have sprouted from the gorgon Medusa's blood when the Greek hero Perseus beheaded her (see Chapter 10), coral branches were mounted on drinking cups so they could be plunged into beverages to eliminate toxins. Artisans also crafted gilded cups in the shape of a "sea unicorn," with the head and torso of a unicorn and a vessel made from the pearly, curly shell of a turban snail. Before drinking, royal personages could unscrew the front and back of the ornate device and dip the unicorn's horn into the shell-cup.

What Lies Beneath a Unicorn's Horn?

Back in 332 B.C.E., Queen Amanirenas (or Candace as the Europeans called her) of Ethiopia (which at that time comprised much of East Africa) supposedly sent Alexander the Great a unicorn as a gift. According to legend, the queen didn't consider the unicorn's horn with its fabled magical properties valuable. What nestled at the base of that spiral-shaped spear mattered more: a precious and priceless ruby (or carbuncle). The twelfth-century German poet and cleric, Pfaffen Lamprecht immortalized the story in his epic poem "Song of Alexander" (see Chapter 5).

The medieval alchemists also saw a connection between the carbuncle/ruby and the unicorn's horn. They believed the carbuncle could neutralize toxins and purify whatever it touched—and that the gem could be found on the unicorn's forehead at the base of its horn. Wolfram von Eschenbach, the most significant epic poet of Germany during the late twelfth and early thirteenth centuries, wrote:

> "We caught the beast called Unicorn
> That knows and loves a maiden best
> And falls asleep upon her breast;
> We took from underneath his horn
> The splendid male carbuncle stone
> Sparkling against the white skull-bone."

The Unicorn Cup's Symbolism

According to psychoanalyst C.G. Jung, who spent a lot of time examining symbols, the cup fabricated from a unicorn's horn represented both masculine and feminine principles, and united the two forces. The horn, of course, is a phallic symbol whereas the cup signifies the womb. Additionally, in the Christian sacrament of Communion, the cup/chalice holds wine to symbolize the blood of Christ that purifies sin.

The Nourishing Horn

Not only does the unicorn's horn possess the power to purify contaminated water, it can also produce water. One legend tells us that the unicorn plunged his horn into a rock, and from that rock sprang the waters of life. It's said that wherever these waters flow, the land will bloom with vitality and fruitfulness, and the animals will be nourished.

According to *De Historia et Veritate Unicornis*, however, when the nurturing water burst forth from the barren rock, it also seeped deep into the earth and trickled down through the crevices, into the hidden caverns below. There, the life-giving waters created fertile ground and spawned a terrible dragon, a dragon who represented the force of darkness and who forevermore would be the righteous unicorn's nemesis.

Wine Instead of Water

At the Château de Pommard winery in Burgundy, France, a bronze unicorn stabs his horn into a brick wall in order to produce red wine. The sculpture, created by the noted twentieth-century artist Salvador Dalí, graces the Court Square of the eighteenth-century castle where the winery is located.

The Unicorn's Intuitive Powers

Sprouting as it does from the unicorn's brow, the horn also suggests a connection with mystical power and clairvoyance. Eastern philosophy describes seven major energy centers in the body, called the "chakras," where the Divine intersects with the human body. Acupuncturists, Reiki practitioners, and other holistic healers address the chakras in their healing practices. Sensitive individuals see the chakras as swirling light. The area on your forehead, between your eyebrows at the top of your nose, is known as the *ajna* or brow chakra.

Western mystical traditions also consider the "third eye" to be the center of psychic perception—our connection to subtle fields of intelligence and the higher realms of existence. Among other things, the unicorn is renowned for his abilities to communicate intuitively and to determine instantly the purity of the people he meets, abilities related directly to his prominent horn and its position.

"If you see a unicorn in a dream or vision, it may tell you to keep the faith—don't give up. A unicorn could also advise you to be more gentle and kind. Encountering a unicorn might warn you to trust your intuition, not just your intellect."

—Skye Alexander, *The Secret Power of Spirit Animals*

WILD AND FREE

Despite millennia of speculation about unicorns, none of these fanciful beasts has ever been captured (other than a few flukes) and no scientific proof of the creature's existence on earth has ever turned up. No DNA samples. No evidence to carbon-date. Not even any legitimate photographs. Like other mythical beings, the unicorn lives "between the worlds" and never totally enmeshes himself in our earthly realm, although he may come here to visit from time to time.

Legends agree that this magnificent beast must live wild and unfettered in order to survive. Some tales say that if you trap a unicorn and cut off his horn, he'll die. In modern times, the unicorn has become emblematic of independence, of all things rare and unique, and of the right to choose your own path regardless of how unconventional it may be.

Only those humans who are pure in body, mind, heart, and spirit can commune with unicorns. You can't bluff a unicorn. Its superior intellect and psychic powers enable it to read the future as well as the thoughts of its own kind and of humans too—and thereby escape the traps set to ensnare it. Only when the unicorn encounters innocence and purity equal to its own, will it surrender its freedom and lay its head in the mythical virgin's lap. Only love, it seems, can win over the unicorn. Love, kindness, and beauty are what keep us in the game and make us believe that life matters.

The Unicorn in Captivity

The famous Renaissance tapestry titled *The Unicorn in Captivity*, which now hangs in the Cloisters of New York's Metropolitan Museum of Art, depicts a unicorn enclosed within a fence, his golden collar attached to a tree. He has succumbed to love, but at what price? Again, we see a parallel between the unicorn and the love-struck knight of the medieval and Renaissance eras.

THE IMMORTAL UNICORN

Immortality is a common feature of mythical creatures, such as mermaids, dragons, and fairies. Perhaps because they can appear and disappear at will, and their bodies lack permanent substance, they aren't locked into the "fourscore and ten" by which we humans must abide. Such is the case with the unicorn. It's speculated that a unicorn can live hundreds, or even thousands of years—unless hunters manage to trap and kill it, or cut off its famous horn. Robert Graves, in his landmark 1993 book *The White Goddess*, proposed that immortality comes through wisdom and integrity. Thus, it is the unicorn's purity that enables it to live forever.

It's not much of a stretch to think that an immortal creature might also be able to convey life-saving energy to other beings. Many stories say that if the unicorn touches an ailing person with its horn, that person will be healed. But human fear and greed sometimes spur extreme or even cruel measures in an attempt to acquire that precious, life-giving power.

Remember the legend encapsulated at the beginning of Chapter 1? The unicorn is a sacred creature, and the king forbids his soldiers to harm it. Spilling its blood is considered a gross evil and a crime against not only the animal kingdom, but against the order of the universe. Yet, the belief that the unicorn's blood contains magical healing properties—even immortality—can lead desperate individuals down evil paths. Perhaps this concept shows another example of the early Christian connection between the unicorn and Christ, who we're told healed the sick and raised the dead.

In J.K. Rowling's novel and the subsequent movie *Harry Potter and the Sorcerer's Stone*, unicorn blood is described as a thick, silver-colored liquid with the power to keep someone who drinks it alive—as evil Lord Voldemort did. Killing a unicorn, however, was known to place a horrible curse on the person who drank its blood. "The blood of a unicorn will keep you alive, even if you are an inch from death, but at a terrible price," the centaur Firenze explains to Harry. "You have slain something pure and defenseless to save yourself, and you will have but a half-life, a cursed life, from the moment the blood touches your lips."

What Makes a Magic Wand Magical?

According to J.K. Rowling in her Harry Potter stories, some of the most powerful magic wands contain a secret ingredient: unicorn hair. The purity of the unicorn lends both clarity and consistency to the wand's magic, so that spells cast with it are unlikely to go askew. Such wands are also reputed to be faithful to their owners and resistant to the powers of the Dark Arts, for they embody the unicorn's traits of loyalty and honesty.

The website Gods and Monsters (*www.gods-and-monsters.com*) points out that among the many supernatural creatures we meet in mythology, the unicorn may be the only one that isn't fearsome. Dragons, mermaids, fairies, and other mythic beings all have their dark sides—and they can be dangerous if crossed. But despite the unicorn's ability to inflict injury with its massive horn, it never attacks people or other creatures unless they attack it first. Instead, unicorns serve the good and offer help to all, humans and animals alike.

THE UNICORN'S DOMESTIC LIFE

Folklore tells us that unicorns prefer to live in small groups—although these may not be comprised of family members. Sometimes an elder unicorn or mature mated pair presides over the group, offering wisdom and counsel to the youngsters. Reclusive creatures, they prefer to abide in quiet, harmonious situations and eschew conflict, chaos, and complications of all kinds.

"The unicorn holds many secrets: the secrets of jungles and moonlight, the secrets which lie hidden at the roots of trees and conceal themselves in coral labyrinths beneath the ocean. I look deep into its amber eyes and see my own reflection, but altered in line and light, as if in a dream."

—Josephine Bradley, *In Pursuit of the Unicorn*

The Unicorn's Diet

Accounts differ about what unicorns eat. Some lore tells us that unicorns, like cattle and deer, subsist largely on grass and moss—a theory based on reports from people who claim to have seen unicorns nuzzling along the forest floor. An old English nursery rhyme says they'll eat white bread or brown, but would really rather have plum cake. French naturalist Alfred Duvaucel swore they ate squirrels, rabbits, and partridges, which they speared with their sharp horns. In James Thurber's fable "The Unicorn in the Garden," a unicorn breakfasts on roses, tulips, and lilies. Jessica Marquis, in her humorous book *Raising Unicorns: Your Step-by-Step Guide to Starting and Running a Successful—and Magical!—Unicorn Farm*, points out that health-conscious unicorns prefer kale.

Another tale says that these mystical creatures don't need to eat anything at all. Instead, they gain nourishment and energy from the sun's light, which they can absorb into their bodies—perhaps through their amazing horns. We really don't know. No one to date has performed an autopsy on a unicorn and checked out the contents of its stomach.

Where Do Little Unicorns Come From?

Again, legends conflict when it comes to the unicorn's reproductive practices. According to some sources, unicorns mature between the ages of thirty and forty. When it's time to start thinking about starting a family, the unicorns leave their childhood homes and go off into the wilderness to find partners. Like other animals and some human beings, the males tend to become more aggressive at this time—especially when competing for mates.

Being rather particular creatures, unicorns don't rush into relationships and may spend years looking for Mr. or Ms. Right. When a unicorn does finally meet a suitable partner, the two take their time getting to know one another, because they will stay together for the rest of their very long lives. After mating, the female is pregnant for about two and a half years—but she doesn't show it until just before the baby's birth. Like wild deer and antelope infants, baby unicorns can stand and even run soon after being born.

Another theory, however, ties into the Christian myth of virgin birth. This version says that unicorns don't mate in the usual, physical way and females can't conceive or give birth. According to Santerian mythology, the Goddess Avá dreams new unicorns into being, and adult unicorn couples adopt the "virgin-born" babies.

The Maiden and the Unicorn, Domenichino 1602

WHERE CAN YOU SEE A UNICORN?

ou probably won't spot a unicorn in Times Square or under the Arc de Triomphe or at the Taj Mahal. Nor will you find one at your local shopping mall or football stadium. Because of its elusive and solitary nature, the unicorn prefers to reside in remote areas where people and the busyness of everyday life won't interrupt its peace and quiet. Centuries ago, you may have had a better chance of sighting this shy, woodland creature that lives apart from the hustle and bustle of human existence, but in our modern world that opportunity has decreased dramatically.

Ted Andrews, author of *Treasures of the Unicorn: The Return to the Sacred Quest*, claims to have seen a unicorn himself. "Unicorns are difficult to see," he writes. "They live at the edges of the mind and in the corners of the eyes. They are often sighted near waterfalls and in meadows of flowers—especially at dawn, while the dew remains upon the grass. They can also be seen during the wondrous time of twilight, as if bathing in the last sprays of sun in preparation for the moonlight dance . . . "

According to James Huneker in his book *Unicorns*, "He dwells in equivocal twilights; and he can stare the sun out of countenance. The enchanting Unicorn boasts no favoured zone. He runs around the globe. He is of all ages and climes."

If you really want to see a unicorn, you'll need to follow the advice that Matthew Webber gives in "Hunting Unicorns" on his website *www.unicorn-dream.co.uk*.

"Go somewhere wild and remote—a forest, a desert, moorland or prairie. Take nothing that might distract you: leave behind the cell phone and the GPS. Wear casual, comfortable clothing, preferably not leather or fur. Wear no scent but your own. Let your thoughts be your own—drink and drugs repel your quarry. Stand and listen, and let the atmosphere permeate you. Forget the trivial concerns of human existence and feel what matters: the life around you; the movement of the air; the scent of the ground . . . Don't let nature humble you: acknowledge that you are a part of it and take pride in that belonging. Feel. Believe. In such a way might you sense the presence of a Unicorn. A presence at once bold and timid; ancient and youthful; full of wisdom and naive as a child. Seldom seen and never heard, he will nuzzle at your soul. Don't seek to touch him or possess him. Acknowledge that you have been noticed by a Wonder."

"The writers of the stories that follow know magic is tough, love hard and demanding, and unicorns not as easy as some of us might like to think; neither safe, nor sweet nor simple. Following the unicorn path requires all the strength, patience, and courage you can muster. Unicorns expect sacrifice from those who love them—and from those they love in return. But if your heart is bold and your spirit true, the rewards can be great indeed. Downright glorious, in fact."

—Bruce Coville, *A Glory of Unicorns*

PART II

UNICORNS THROUGH THE AGES

CHAPTER 4

Unicorns of the Ancient World

"When God created the earth, He made a river which flowed from the Garden of Eden . . . Then God told Adam to name the animals . . . And the first animal he named was the unicorn. When the Lord heard the name Adam had spoken, he reached down and touched the tip of the single horn growing from the animal's forehead. From that moment on, the unicorn was elevated above other beasts."

—Nancy Hathaway, *The Unicorn*

HOW LONG HAVE unicorns been around? Some myths say forever, even before the earth emerged from the Void. Other legends suggest that they may have lived on our planet hundreds of thousands, maybe millions of years ago, but have since become extinct. We do know that for millennia people around the world have wondered about them, told stories about them, revered and loved them, and fashioned art portraying them in various fanciful forms.

CAVE PAINTINGS OF UNICORNS

More than 15,000 years ago, unknown artists painted thousands of colorful images of animals and people, as well as abstract designs, on the walls of the prehistoric caves at Lascaux, in the south of France. Researchers have since identified approximately 600 of these pictures as representing deer, bison, bears, cattle, horses, and other familiar animals. But among these ancient records of earth's animal species appears a creature with a single horn jutting from its forehead . . . is it the fabled unicorn?

Possibly the mysterious animal is actually a type of deer, antelope, or bovine creature, but because of the perspective from which the artist represented it, the animal's two horns appear as one. That's a popular theory today. Kenyan anthropologist Dr. Richard Leakey, however, suggests that the image may show a *therianthrope*, a hybrid mythic figure, rather than an actual animal. Folklore contains many tales of blended beings and deities who possess the features of more than one species. Shamans in earlier times often wore animal skins and horns during rituals intended to connect with the spirits of the animals.

However, that doesn't discount the possibility that the unidentified horned creature did, in fact, exist all those years ago, and has since become extinct. At least that's what English travel writer Bruce Chatwin noted in his 1977 book *In Patagonia*. Chatwin shares with his readers the ideas of Manuel Jesus Molina, a priest who told him the rock art at Lago Posadas, Argentina, depicted unicorns that had lived there and were hunted by men for thousands of years. Chatwin also mentioned a painting at Cerro del Indio, of a bulky one-horned beast whose ancient portrait is too indistinct to provide an accurate ID. Nearby, a World Heritage Site of the UNESCO known as the Cave of the Hands, shows another single-horned animal among the other petroglyphs.

UNICORNS OF PERSIA AND ASSYRIA

xcavations at Susa, in Iran, one of the world's oldest cities dating back some 5,000 years, have turned up artwork depicting unicorns. Archaeologists also found unicorn bas-reliefs and sculptures at Nineveh, the oldest city in the ancient Assyrian Empire. Additionally, they discovered carved stones and cylinders featuring unicorns that were used as seals to mark property or as insignia of important people.

Unicorns, though, didn't just serve as decorative elements for ancient artists. These mystical beasts also appear in the sacred texts of Zoroastrianism. Founded 3,500 years ago, Zoroastrianism was the official religion of Persia from 600 B.C.E. to C.E. 650. One passage, translated in Pulitzer Prize-winner Odell Shepard's 1930 book *The Lore of the Unicorn*, shows an obvious reverence for the unicorn: "We worship the Good Mind and the spirits of the Saints

and the sacred beast the Unicorn which stands in Vouru-Kasha, and we sacrifice to that sea of Vouru-Kasha where he stands."

Religious writings also refer to an unusual type of ass, described as having only three legs, that purified the waters of the sea Varkash so that the "good" animals could drink. This belief in the unicorn's power to purify tainted water lasted for thousands of years, and continued to flourish throughout the cultures of medieval and Renaissance Europe.

UNICORNS ACCORDING TO THE ANCIENT GREEKS

The ancient Greeks had plenty of mythology, rich with tales of colorful deities and all sorts of unusual creatures. However, unicorns don't appear there among the centaurs and the Chimaera. Why? Because the Greeks thought the unicorn was a real animal and they recorded information about it in books of natural history instead of folklore.

Visions of Unicorns

About 2,500 years ago, the Greek historian and physician Ctesias spent an extended period of time in Persia, where he was privy to numerous mystical tales from the Middle East and beyond. While there, he wrote about the unicorn in his book *Indica* (a history of India). He described the creature as having a white body, a purple head, blue eyes, and a red, black, and white horn between twenty-five and thirty inches long. According to Ctesias, the unicorn was a type of wild ass as large as a horse that lived in the distant and mysterious land of India. He also mentioned that "the dust filed from this horn is administered in a potion as a protection against deadly drugs." Might this be the origin of the belief among medieval Europeans that the unicorn's horn could neutralize poison?

Although most accounts describe the unicorn as docile and peace loving, Ctesias claimed that it was "one of the strongest of all creatures, and so fleet that neither a horse nor any other animal can overtake it. When it is pursued, it first runs leisurely, but later it increases its speed. It defends itself with its horn, teeth, and hoofs, and often slays many horses and men."

In the following century, the great Greek philosopher Aristotle validated Ctesias's statements. He wrote that only a few animals with a solid hoof and one horn existed, those being the Indian ass and the African oryx. A few centuries later, Strabo, a noted geographer and historian of the time, claimed that one-horned horses with heads like stags lived in the Caucasus (a region on the border of Europe and Asia, between the Black and Caspian Seas).

Curiouser and Curiouser

About 1,800 years ago, a Greek scholar named Aelian wrote a book titled *On the Nature of Animals*. Apparently, Aelian based some of the curious stories he included in the book on his predecessors' suppositions, for he wrote that "wild asses" roamed India, as Ctesias had claimed 700 years before him. In fact, Aelian described the wondrous creatures in almost the same way Ctesias did, considering that he had no personal knowledge of the magical beasts.

The Abduction of Prosperine, Albrecht Dürer 1516

"I have found that wild asses as large as horses are to be found in India. The body of this animal is white, except on the head, which is red, while the eyes are azure. It has a horn on the brow, about one cubit and a half in length, which is white at the base, crimson at the top, and black between. These variegated horns are used as drinking cups by the Indians . . . It is said that whosoever drinks from this kind of horn is safe from all incurable diseases such as convulsions and the so-called holy disease [epilepsy], and that he cannot be killed by poison."

How Much Is a Cubit?

This ancient measurement varies, due to the fact that it's based on the length of a man's forearm, from the bend at the elbow to the end of the middle finger. Generally speaking, at the time people used this measurement, a cubit equaled about 1.5 feet.

Elsewhere Ctesias claimed that unicorns resided deep in the heart of India where no man could go, and where all manner of wild beasts roamed. He called the unicorn a *kartajan*, which means "Lord of the desert" in Sanskrit. This time he described it as standing as tall as a horse with a single black horn, a tawny coat, a goat's tail, and an elephant's feet. Although Aelian said that the unicorns fought among themselves, they played nicely with other creatures and preferred the solitude of desolate places to hanging out in crowds.

Of course, as we now know, the oryx and the blackbuck antelope—which lived in those regions and may have been taken for unicorns—have two horns, not one, and animals with red-white-and-black horns probably exist only in little girls' bed-rooms. So where did these learned men get their information? It's unlikely that they had firsthand knowledge of the unicorns they described—Ctesias never traveled to India and Strabo visited only a few of the places he wrote about (the Caucasus area probably wasn't one of them).

What's interesting is that they truly believed such an amazing creature lived on our planet. Aristotle insisted that just because he hadn't actually seen a unicorn up close and personal didn't mean that unicorns didn't exist. After all, he'd never seen elephants or giraffes either. Because these scholars were held in such high esteem during their time, their conviction lent credence to the uni-corn's existence, and their visions of unicorns influenced our ideas for centuries.

> "There are many things which reason cannot account for, and are nevertheless true."
>
> —Augustine of Hippo, *City of God* (C.E. 426)

The Only Man to Ride a Unicorn

During his campaigns in the third century B.C.E., Alexander the Great—who at that time was considered a descendant of the gods, maybe even a god himself—rode a magnificent horse named Bucephalus. But legends say that Bucephalus wasn't a mere horse: he was a unicorn. His name, for instance, means "ox-headed" and suggests that the beast sported horns. Additionally, the animal had a reputation for being untamable—he was so wild and ferocious that Alexander's father wanted to have the creature killed. But the young Alexander recognized magic when he saw it, and stepped in to save Bucephalus—and the two bonded for life. Both classical and medieval manuscripts describe Alexander as riding a unicorn. Perhaps Bucephalus's superior powers even helped Alexander achieve his incredible success as a conqueror. How cool is that?

Alexander never actually claimed to have ridden or even seen a unicorn in the flesh, nor do any of the other ancient writers whose imaginations shaped our early views of these illustrious beasts. Most of them, it seems, simply extrapolated on what their literate fellows had proposed earlier.

Alexander's countryman, a merchant named Cosmas Indicopleustes, based his interpretation of unicorns on sculptures that he said guarded the palace of the king of Ethiopia. In his sixth-century *Christian Topography* he recounted tales of the unicorn's strength and dexterity. If hunters pursued the unicorn, he explained, it dove off a cliff and landed on its shock-absorbing, springy horn, thus escaping its enemies.

THE ROMAN VIEW OF UNICORNS

The ancient Romans adopted and adapted many of Greece's ideas—including those concerning the unicorn. Like their Greek neighbors, the Romans considered the unicorn a flesh-and-blood creature, rather than a mythological being. Pliny the Elder, a first-century Roman philosopher and author of the encyclopedia *Natural History*, spoke of a wild, fierce beast he called a *monoceros* with "a stag's head, elephant's feet, and a boar's tail, the rest of its body being like that of a horse. It makes a deep lowing noise, and one black horn two cubits long projects from the middle of its forehead. This animal, they say, cannot be taken alive."

Furthermore, Pliny stated that the peculiar creature could change its color. Was he describing a rhinoceros, some other wild animal . . . or perhaps a unicorn? Most likely, he and others who came before and after him took a little of this and a little of that, combining folklore and speculation—and maybe even a bit of foolery from native sources—to come up with a conception of a convoluted imaginary creature.

THE UNICORN IN GERMANY

According to the Roman emperor Julius Caesar (100–44 B.C.E.), if you wanted to spot a unicorn you should go to the Hercynian Forest (part of what is now known as the Black Forest) in Germany. In his book *Commentaries on the Gallic Wars*, Caesar described unicorns, along with other awe-inspiring creatures, as living in this dense, dark forest, which provided the ideal setting for all sorts of mysterious and magical happenings. Immense in scale, the forest by Caesar's calculations was nine days' journey in breadth and sixty days' in depth. It stretched along the Danube and Rhine Rivers to Transylvania and beyond, including parts of what we now know as Southern Germany, Austria, and Hungary. But he added the caveat that no one really knew where the forest ended. On this deliciously frightening stage, many German fairy tales and legends have played out over the centuries, including those concerning the unicorn.

When Is an Ox Not an Ox?

Romans had a tendency to lump large animals into the category of *boves* meaning "oxen." Elephants, rhinos, bison, and even seals fell under this heading. Consequently, some of these early writers' comments confuse the unicorn issue, to say the least.

ANCIENT CHINESE UNICORNS

In the Chinese myth of the Creation, in the beginning the universe was a giant egg. Then one day, the egg cracked and everything went to pieces. The god P'an Ku spent the next 18,000 years sorting things out, along with the help of four magical animals: the dragon, the phoenix, the tortoise, and the unicorn. When P'an Ku was satisfied with his work, he died and his animal aides assumed their rightful realms. The dragon dove into the ocean; the tortoise lumbered into the earthbound swamps and marshes; the phoenix soared high into the sky; and the unicorn dashed off to the woodlands. To this day, the four sacred creatures can be viewed as ambassadors of four of the Chinese elements water, earth, fire, and wood, as well as the earthly regions that represent them physically.

An Age of Peace and Prosperity

Legend tells us that in 2697 B.C.E. an unusual animal wandered into the palace of the Chinese emperor Huang-ti, also known as the Yellow Emperor. This unique creature had the body of a horse, the head of a dragon, and was known as a *qilin* (or *k'i-lin*). According to some accounts, the splendid being radiated all the colors of the rainbow, and its voice rang out like a thousand wind chimes. A prodigious horn protruded twelve feet from its forehead, and when it walked, its graceful feet made no sound. Peace loving and docile, the qilin eschewed violence and would do just about anything to avoid a fight—perhaps for that reason, it had a lifespan of a thousand years.

The emperor considered the animal a sign of good luck and prosperity for his country. Indeed, during Huang-ti's reign the Chinese advanced considerably, creating musical instruments and building houses from brick. The unicorn's gentle nature is said even to have inspired China's Golden Age of Peace. During Huang-ti's final days, the unicorn returned to the palace to carry the beloved emperor on its back to the land of the dead.

Omen of Change

Chinese legends say that the unicorn appears whenever a wise, just, and powerful ruler is about to be born or die.

The Zhi

A one-horned animal found in Chinese folklore called the *zhi* (also referred to as the *xie zhi*) was believed to possess incredible psychic powers. Legends tell us that the zhi lived in China during the early Han dynasty (circa 200 B.C.E.), where it sat in on court trials and offered legal assistance to court officials. Being a pure and guileless creature itself, it could see straight into the souls of other beings—humans as well as animals—and could instantly determine whether they were innocent or guilty. If it decided someone was guilty, it meted out a quick and sure punishment: It gored the criminal through the heart with its horn.

In earlier times, officials of the Chinese court wore an image of the zhi on their clothing to distinguish them and their rank. Even in modern times, the symbol for the zhi appears in the Chinese character *fa*, meaning "law."

The Beginning of the *Bagua*

Two centuries earlier, the qilin was said to have appeared to the Chinese sovereign Fu Hsi while he sat beside the Yellow River. The qilin emerged from the river, right before Fu Hsi's eyes. Although it resembled a horse, the creature had shining scales like those of a dragon. As the man gazed at the qilin, he noticed unusual symbols covering its back and he scribbled them into the sand with a stick. These symbols provided the information Fu Hsi needed to invent the first written Chinese language.

The symbols are still known today as the *bagua* (or *pa kua*). The eight, three-lined figures called "trigrams" are made up of broken and unbroken lines. In addition to serving as the inspiration for a written form of communication, the trigrams also form the basis of the ancient divination system known as the *I Ching* or *Book of Changes* and play a role in the Chinese art of placement called *feng shui.*

Confucius and the Qilin

In 550 B.C.E. a young Chinese woman named Yen Chen-tsai had a fortuitous encounter with a unicorn. She and her husband wanted a son but had not managed to produce one, which distressed the couple greatly. After many years, Yen Chen-tsai decided to visit a holy shrine in the mountains. Along the way, she met a qilin, who gave her a small jade tablet engraved with the words: "The son of the essence of water shall succeed to the withering Chou and he will become a throneless king." As the qilin predicted, the woman gave birth to a son whom she named Kung Fu Tse, which means "the essence of water." We know him today as Confucius.

Seventy years later, the great sage heard that a group of noblemen had killed an unusual animal. Confucius hurried to the scene and recognized the dead beast as the qilin. Legend tells us that, as a result of the incident, he stopped writing forever—and from that day, it's said, no one ever again saw a qilin.

> "In the age of Tang and Yu the Unicorn
> and the Phoenix walked abroad.
> Now when it is not their time they come
> And what do they seek?
> The Unicorn, the Unicorn, my heart is sad."
> —Confucius

CHAPTER 5

Medieval Unicorns

"[I]t is marvelously clear that when the unicorn was first described and centuries later when the tapestries were woven, everyone believed in unicorns."

—Marianna Mayer, *The Unicorn and the Lake*

UNICORNS REACHED THEIR height of popularity—until modern times, that is—during the medieval period, an era that spans nearly a millennium between the fall of Rome in Europe in C.E. 475 until the start of the Renaissance in the fourteenth century. It's no surprise that unicorns and other incredible creatures captured the imaginations of Europeans at the time. Also referred to as the Dark Ages, this was a period of mystery and superstition, intense religious fervor, and curiosity about the world beyond what was commonly known.

Adventurers began exploring faraway and exotic lands—India, Arabia, Africa, and the South Seas—and returned brimming with tales of strange creatures and incredible experiences. Legends and fables from numerous cultures infiltrated the folklore of the Europeans. Sailors claimed to have seen mermaids riding the waves of the vast oceans. Travelers along the Silk Road spoke of fire-breathing dragons, giants, and terrifying human-animal hybrids. Although people's imaginations had always held conceptions of bizarre beings—divine and otherwise—the stories brought back from foreign lands enriched and expanded upon the ideas Europeans had previously entertained.

MEDIEVAL BESTIARIES

During medieval times, people in Europe and the Middle East were fascinated with tales about animals—not merely the wild and domesticated ones they encountered in their daily lives, but mythical creatures as well. The Old Testament of the Bible mentioned animals, including unicorns, in ways that gave them spiritual significance—and because the Bible told them so, people accepted it. Additionally, our ancestors believed that God intended for animals to teach humans. For example, in Job 12:7–8, King James Version, we find the passage: "But ask now the beasts, and they shall teach thee; and the fowls of the air, and they shall tell thee. Or speak to the earth, and it shall teach thee; and the fishes of the sea shall declare unto thee."

Animals as Allegories

Sometime around the third century, a book called the *Physiologus* presented a collection of about fifty stories that used animals and birds as Christian allegories. Over time, more animal tales were added, based on Indian, Hebrew, and Egyptian legends, and the text was translated from the original Greek into all the major languages of Europe. The collection became so popular that only the Bible could claim a larger reading audience. In the seventh century, Isidore of Seville wrote an encyclopedia called the *Etymologiae*, which contained animal lore and material drawn in part from the works of earlier authors, including the noted first-century Roman philosopher Pliny the Elder. The two texts were later combined to form what became known as a *Book of Beasts* or *Bestiary*.

Bestiaries weren't intended to be accurate scientific or zoological resources. Instead, they served as moral guides for the faithful and offered Christian interpretations of the animals, including the unicorn, that were mentioned in the Bible. The twelfth-century *Aberdeen Bestiary* said its purpose was "to improve the minds of ordinary people, in such a way that the soul will at least perceive physically things which it has difficulty grasping mentally." The bestiaries also presented information about the creatures of the world—fanciful as well as real—that captured the public's imagination at the time.

Because the medieval masses were generally illiterate, artists illustrated the bestiaries. Pictures of both unicorns and monoceroses turn up on these vellum pages, along with descriptions of the beasts. For example, the *Aberdeen Bestiary* tells us, "The monoceros is a monster with a horrible bellow, the body of a horse, the feet of an elephant and a tail very like that of a deer. A magnificent, marvelous horn projects from the middle of its forehead, four feet in length, so sharp that whatever it strikes is easily pierced with the blow. No living monoceros has ever come into man's hands, and while it can be killed, it cannot be captured."

Numerous bestiaries included paintings of both unicorns and monoceroses, which suggests that people considered them to be two different species. Some creatures appear to have been based on the rhinoceros. Others feature the heads of dogs or monkeys, scales, spiky backs, striped coats, and dragon-like or serpent-like character- istics. Although the monoceros stands alone in many of these depic- tions, the unicorn is usually shown with its head resting in the lap of a woman while hunters attack it with spears, swords, and axes. That's because in these morality stories, the unicorn symbolizes Christ and the soldiers represent the Jews who crucified him.

Bestiaries for Lovers

Some popular bestiaries provided guidance in matters of love and relationships. In the era of courtly love (beginning around the eleventh century, see Chapter 1), a strict set of rules governed romantic endeavors. Authors and artists used animals in the bes- tiaries to convey specific meanings and instructions for lovers, symbolically drawing on the attributes people associated with the beasts and birds. For example, a fox represented cunning and trick- ery; an eagle stood for courage; a stag indicated vanity; a panther signified the sorrows of love. Bards and troubadours incorporated animals into their poems and songs, not only for entertainment but for their listeners' edification as well.

The unicorn, in these works, usually symbolized the male suitor who surrendered his wild independence and gave himself over to love. One of the best known of the lyric poets of the time, the thirteenth-century French *chansonnier* Thibaut IV of Champagne, described himself as a bedazzled unicorn in his "Licorne de Thibaut de Champagne." In the song, he likens himself to the hunted beast who is slain by love.

"The unicorn and I are one:
He also pauses in amaze
Before some maiden's magic gaze,
And while he wonders, is undone.
On some dear breast he slumbers deep
And Treason slays him in that sleep.
Just so have ended my Life's days;
So Love and my Lady lay me low.
My heart will not survive this blow."

In some tales, however, the unicorn not only becomes the captive of the lady he loves, he also takes an active role in pursuing her—thus, he fills both roles of hunter and hunted. Such songs describe the maiden as being tied naked to a tree in the forest, where the unicorn seduces her before he's killed. The symbolism may suggest the *petite mort* (little death), which refers to orgasm.

A Picture's Worth a Thousand Words

To help the faithful remember their priests' sermons, medieval churches throughout Europe and the British Isles incorporated bestiary images into their very structures, both inside and out. Unicorns and other mythic creatures were carved on pews and altar furniture, rendered in stone on walls and friezes, pieced together in mosaics and stained glass windows, and woven into tapestries. For example, unicorns have their place in the stained glass windows of the Basilica Cathedral of Saint-Denis near Paris; Amiens Cathedral in France; the castle chapel at Ebreichsdorf, Austria; St. Giles Cathedral in Edinburgh, Scotland; King's College Chapel in Cambridge, England, and many more. Although the art of making stained glass dates back to ancient Rome, it reached a height during the late medieval/Gothic period (circa 1150–1500).

Architectural Unicorns

Many buildings today, secular as well as sacred, still feature unicorns as motifs in their architecture. In Boston, for example, a silver unicorn and a golden lion perch atop the city's Old State House, the oldest public building remaining from the original thirteen colonies in America. Unicorns greet visitors at the entrances to Ottawa's Parliament Building, Scotland's Parliament Building, the Tower of London, and the Governor's Palace in Williamsburg, Virginia. Their visages inspire students at King's College in Aberdeen, Scotland, and at the Russian State University for the Humanities (formerly the Synod Printing House where the first book in Russian was printed in 1564). Countless other structures, including churches, businesses, and even apartment buildings depict the unicorn prominently, using its image as a form of sympathetic magic to attract the fabled beast's well-known qualities of good fortune, strength, and longevity.

Toward the end of the Middle Ages, other texts featuring animals, both domestic and exotic, started appearing. Among the most famous was *Aesop's Fables*, which we still enjoy today. Although these fables lacked specific Christian metaphors, they offered moral guidance. In one story, "The Lion and the Unicorn," the innocent unicorn has compassion even for his long-time enemy, the lion. When the ailing, old lion asks if he can borrow the unicorn's horn to use as a walking stick, the kindhearted unicorn agrees and loans his horn—his only weapon—to the lion. Naturally, the lion then attacks the defenseless beast. The tale's moral was show no mercy; you can't trust your enemy and must always be prepared to defend yourself against him. Expanded encyclopedias spun off from the earlier bestiaries, providing information about zoology, botany, and geography, along with a wide range of other subjects—but without the religious or moral overtones.

UNICORN SIGHTING

One of the most renowned of the medieval travelers, Ahmad Ibn Fadlan (played by Antonio Banderas in the 1999 movie *The Thirteenth Warrior*), described unicorns in his *Risala* (meaning Letters), a journal he kept during his travels in Russia. In it he writes, "Whenever it [the unicorn] sees a rider, it approaches and if the rider has a fast horse, the horse tries to escape by running fast, and if the beast overtakes them, it picks the rider out of the saddle with its horn, and tosses him in the air, and meets him with the point of the horn, and continues doing so until the rider dies. But it will not harm or hurt the horse in any way or manner."

HOW TO CAPTURE A UNICORN

edieval legends claimed that the only way to capture the elusive and untamable unicorn was to take a virgin of noble birth deep into the forest and leave her there to await the sought-after beast's arrival. When the unicorn, smitten by her beauty and innocence, trotted over and laid its head in her lap (or sometimes suckled at her breast), the hunters would pounce upon the animal and slay it.

During the Middle Ages, women were viewed as temptresses and men as helpless victims who, when confronted with the ladies' charms, just couldn't resist them. The Old Testament portrayed Eve as sinful and deceptive because she gave the hapless Adam an apple to eat and got the couple tossed out of Paradise. By extension, the church regarded all women as tainted and suspect. Alluring or powerful women were considered particularly dangerous and often labeled witches. During the reign of the Inquisition in Europe, the height of which lasted from the early thirteenth until the mid-fifteenth centuries, at least tens of thousands and perhaps as many as several million people, most of them women and girls (depending on which source you choose to believe) were deemed witches and put to death.

In such an environment of fear, religious domination, and hostility toward females, it's not surprising that girls and women would be used as bait for the rare and incredibly valuable unicorn. At that time, the magnificent beast was always considered to be male, and the fact that only a maiden could tame him simply reinforced the belief that she must have bewitched him. Once under her spell, the unicorn was rendered helpless. Now hunters could kill the animal and take possession of his magical horn. The unicorn's entrapment also served as a metaphorical warning for men: Women can't be trusted, and if you let your guard down they'll deceive you with their wiles—and like the unicorn, you'll die, dude.

"I had from this rich queen

A beast of proud and noble mien

That bears in his brow the ruby-stone

And yields himself to maids alone.

But few such unicorns are found

On this or any other ground,

And only such are ever captured

As stainless virgins have enraptured.

No man of woman born

Endures the terror of his horn."

—Pfaffen Lamprecht, "Song of Alexander"

How to Cook a Unicorn

On April 1, 2012, the British Library in London announced it had discovered a medieval cookbook that included a recipe for roasting a unicorn. Historians suggested the author was Geoffrey Fule, who cooked in the kitchens of England's Queen Philippa of Hainault in the mid-fourteenth century. In his time, Fule was known for concocting unusual dishes made with out-of-the-ordinary ingredients. His directions for roast unicorn instruct you to first marinade the animal in cloves and garlic, and then roast the meat on a griddle. A colorful drawing in the cookbook's margins shows a whole unicorn stretched out on a grill over a bed of hot coals. Another portrays a serving girl carrying the unicorn's head on a platter to the dining table. A third drawing pictures the remains of the unicorn—hooves, tail, and horn—dumped into a garbage can. The amusing "find" turned out to be an April Fool's joke.

THE MAGICAL ALICON

As we discussed in Chapter 3, our ancestors believed the unicorn's distinctive horn carried magical and medicinal properties—most importantly, the ability to purify water and cure illnesses, ranging from epilepsy to syphilis. The term "alicon" refers to the horn itself as well as to the material of which the horn is composed. At a time when people feared death from poison or contaminated water, it's easy to see why the alicon became a prized commodity.

UNICORN SIGHTING

In the late fourteenth century, the priest Johannes Von Hesse of Utrecht in the Netherlands wrote, "the venomous animals poison the water after the going down of the sun, so that the good animals cannot drink of it; but in the morning after sunrise comes the unicorn, and he, dipping his horn in the stream, expels the poison so that during the daytime the other animals may drink. This as I describe it, I have seen with my own eyes."

If you had the money, you could purchase this precious substance from apothecaries in a powdered form to sprinkle in your drink. If you had more money, you could buy a cup fabricated from alicon, which would purify any liquid you sipped from it. At the time, the nobility drank from goblets and ate with utensils supposedly made from unicorn horns. And if you were a member of a royal family, you might have an entire horn stashed away in a locked vault someplace in the basement of your palace. England's Queen Elizabeth I owned two, worth the price of a whole castle.

In his book *Complete Herbal*, Nicholas Culpeper (1616–1654) advised readers that the unicorn's horn in powdered form was a valuable item for concocting cordials for health purposes.

Another writer on medical matters of the period, James Primerose (d. 1659) in his *Popular Errours* advises his readers to be wary of fake unicorn horns—indicating that there was sufficient trade in these items for Primerose to warn people against purchasing or using them.

Most people, of course, couldn't afford the real deal. As we all know, any time a commodity becomes valued the price escalates—especially if it's an item as rare as a unicorn's horn. Merchants out to capitalize on this fabulous treasure, and unable to get their hands on a genuine horn, turned to an alternative: the narwhal's tusk.

What's the Price of a Unicorn's Horn?

In his June 2013 article "10 Magical Facts about Unicorns" for *Mental Floss Magazine*, Dave Gonzales explains just how precious the alicon was during the Middle Ages and the Renaissance. "At its height, 'unicorn horn' was literally worth 10 times its weight in gold. In 1560, German merchants sold a unicorn horn for an astronomical 90,000 scudi—then about £18,000—to the pope. Pharmacies in London sold powdered unicorn horn as late as 1741."

The narwhal, as discussed in Chapter 2, is a small Arctic whale with a big white tusk—ten feet long or more—that spirals like the fabled unicorn's horn. Most of the alicons proffered during the Middle Ages were probably narwhal's tusks, although rhinos, walruses, elephants, and other large beasts were hunted for their "horns" too. After a while, suspicion began to raise its ugly head, as people questioned the validity of the product for which they were shelling out fortunes. Consequently, scientists of the period established a series of "tests" to verify so-called unicorn horns:

- Put the horn in water. If the horn is real, the water will look as though it's boiling except that the water remains cold.
- Put some powdered horn and a scorpion under a bowl. If the scorpion dies, the horn is real.
- With the tip of the horn, draw a circle on the floor and set a spider within the circle. The spider won't be able to get out of the circle if the horn that drew it is authentic.
- Burn some powdered horn—if it's real, it will smell sweet.
- A genuine unicorn horn will sweat when it comes near poison.
- Feed poison to a pigeon, and then give the bird some powdered horn to eat. If the horn is real, the pigeon will survive.

"Very simple men think of the power of a horned beast as residing in the horns with which it defends itself and attacks its enemies; to such men, therefore, horns are a natural symbol of vigour, power, strength of any kind, and they have been used as such a symbol for ages."

—Odell Shepard, *The Lore of the Unicorn*

THE HEALING EINHORN

ince ancient times, people believed unicorns lived in Germany, where they were known as *Einhornen* (meaning one-horned creatures). The Roman emperor Julius Caesar said unicorns could be found in Germany's dense, dark, mysterious Hercynian Forest. Other tales insisted they lived in the Harz Mountains region of central Germany. A cave there called the *Einhornhöhle* was reputed to be the unicorns' lair.

Back in the days when the old gods presided over the land and Germany's vast territory had yet to be mapped, folklore told of a strange, wise, old woman who possessed great curative skills. At this time, forests covered much of Germany, and there the woman lived alone in the Steingrotte Cave near Scharzfeld. People came from all parts of the country in search of her healing ministrations.

Marian Mysticism

Fervent believers in the Einhorn as a symbol for Christ, the German people filled their churches with images of the mythic beast. A branch of German mysticism, based on adoration of the Virgin Mary, referred to Christ's mother as *Maria Unicornis*, or Mary of the Unicorn.

Christian missionaries, however, took issue with her famous powers and pronounced her a witch. They convinced a Frankish king, who happened to be a Christian, to arrest her. The king agreed, and sent soldiers along with a monk to seize the witch. As the king's men approached the old woman at her cave, a unicorn emerged from the dark forest and knelt beside her. She climbed on its back, and the unicorn galloped away.

The soldiers pursued the unicorn, but they couldn't keep up with it—because as everyone knows, the unicorn is the fleetest creature on earth. Only the monk eventually managed to catch up to the pair. But as he tried to drag the woman from the unicorn's back, she waved him away with magical signs. When the soldiers finally reached the monk, they discovered him dead and lying at the bottom of a deep hole in the ground. The old woman and the unicorn had vanished.

"The unicorn is noble;

He keeps him safe and high

Upon a narrow path and steep

Climbing to the sky;

And there no man can take him;

He scorns the hunter's dart

And only a virgin's magic power

Shall tame his haughty heart."

—From a medieval German folksong

UNICORN SIGHTING

During the early part of the thirteenth century, so the tale goes, the great conqueror Genghis Khan decided he'd like to take over India. His army marched southward for many days, subjugating every town they came to—no one could stop them. Finally, they reached the country Khan planned to conquer. But early in the morning before the great battle was to begin, a small, deer-like animal with a green hide and a single, red-and-black horn jutting from its brow approached Kahn. It knelt three times before him, in reverence.

Kahn had heard many tales over the years about the mystical *qilin*, a peace-loving and magical one-horned creature. What could its appearance now mean? As the great warrior gazed into the gentle beast's eyes, he imagined he saw his father looking back at him. Even though his father had died fifty years earlier, Kahn heard the man's voice speaking and sensed him standing nearby. He even smelled his father's scent.

For a few moments, Kahn contemplated the land that lay before him and recalled that this was the birthplace of the Buddha and many Bodhisattvas. Believing the unicorn to be the spirit of his father advising him to cease and desist, the conqueror ordered his soldiers to turn back. The unicorn had rescued India from certain defeat.

CHAPTER 6

Renaissance Unicorns

"The unicorn, through its intemperance and not knowing how to control itself, for the love it bears to fair maidens forgets its ferocity and wildness; and laying aside all fear it will go up to a seated damsel and go to sleep in her lap, and thus the hunters take it."

—Leonardo da Vinci

THE TERM "RENAISSANCE" means rebirth in French, and certainly it seems that during this period, from the fourteenth to the sixteenth centuries, Europe awakened from a millennium of slumber. She shrugged off the somber limitations of the so-called Dark Ages and spread her glorious wings, as human creativity and imagination soared to previously unknown heights. In this time of cultural and intellectual growth art, literature, music, theater, architecture, and scholarship flourished throughout much of Europe. Changes occurred that transformed the Western world forever. Shakespeare penned his enduring works; Columbus sailed to the New World; Copernicus presented a heliocentric model of the solar system; Martin Luther broke with the Roman Catholic Church; the printing press made books and literacy available on a large scale.

But despite all this, the myth of the unicorn and people's fascination with the beguiling beast remained unscathed. If anything, the unicorn's popularity increased, partly due to the explorations of European adventurers into distant territories and partly because of the work of Renaissance artists.

"Towards noon we spotted an animal gazing down at us from a sterile mountain peak of red black rocks. Our guide stated that the animal must certainly be a unicorn, and he pointed out to us the single horn, which jutted from its forehead. With great caution we gazed back at this most noble creature, regretting it was no closer for us to examine."

—Friar Faber, 1438

THE UNICORN TAPESTRIES

The elusive and magical unicorn stars in some of the most famous and treasured works of art that survive from the Renaissance: *The Unicorn Tapestries* a.k.a. *The Hunt for the Unicorn*. Woven of wool, silk, silver, and gilt, probably in Bruges, Belgium between 1495 and 1505, they now hang in the Cloisters of New York's Metropolitan Museum of Art—a gift from John D. Rockefeller Jr. in 1937. Some sources suggest that the tapestries were originally commissioned to mark the wedding of Anne of Brittany to Louis XII, the king of France. The seven ornate panels— twelve feet wide and up to fourteen feet high—depict men hunting the unicorn, much as European aristocrats might have hunted deer in real life, and contain allegorical imagery from both pagan and Christian mythology. (See Chapter 1 for more information.)

The Unicorn Tapestries Revisited

From May 15 until August 18, 2013, New York's Metropolitan Museum of Art celebrated the Cloisters' seventy-fifth anniversary with a special exhibit, Search for the Unicorn. The series of exquisite and intricate late-fifteenth-century tapestries hung on display for twenty-first-century visitors to enjoy. Other treasures in the exhibit included paintings and woodcuts of unicorns, the lavishly illustrated *Hunt for the Unicorn Annunciation Book of Hours*, from Utrecht, Netherlands (circa 1500), 600-year-old sacred texts from the Middle East describing unicorns, and even a rare fifteenth-century German *aquamanile*, a copper unicorn-shaped vessel with a spigot for hand-washing.

The first tapestry panel, *The Hunters Enter the Woods*, shows five men with their dogs and carrying spears as they begin their quest—a quest that endangers their own lives as well as their quarry's. In the second tapestry, *The Unicorn Is Found*, twelve hunters surround the unicorn and a number of other beasts, including some rather odd-looking lions. The animals lie beside a fountain as the unicorn dips its horn into the water to purify it, so that the other creatures may drink safely. The hunters aim their weapons at the unicorn in the third panel, *The Unicorn Is Attacked*, but they can't capture it and it leaps gracefully away from its assailants. In the fourth, *The Unicorn Defends Itself*, the unicorn stabs at its pursuers with its horn and impales one of the hunting dogs. The fifth tapestry, *The Unicorn Is Killed and Brought to the Palace*, shows two images, the unicorn being killed and the lifeless beast slung over the back of a white horse and presented to the king (probably Louis XII, for whom the tapestries were most likely commissioned). *The Mystic Capture of the Unicorn*, the sixth tapestry in the series, depicts the unicorn with its head in the lap of a young woman, an act of naiveté that, according to folklore, has led to its capture.

Perhaps the best known, and the most endearing, is the seventh panel, *The Unicorn in Captivity*. It pictures the snow-white beast corralled in a wooden fence and fastened to a pomegranate tree by a golden chain. (Could this beautiful image have inspired novelist C.S. Lewis's unicorn Jewel, who wore a gold chain in the Narnia stories?) All around the unicorn blossom hundreds of flowers that once were prescribed by Renaissance herbalists to enhance health and fertility. His lovely white coat is stained with red juice from the tree's lush fruit—a medieval symbol of fertility and an apt image to mark the marriage of a noble couple.

Flower Power and the Unicorn

Before the advent of modern pharmaceuticals, people relied on herbal remedies to heal everything from the common cold to infertility. The hundreds of flowers depicted in the unicorn tapestries were known at the time to possess medicinal properties—but more than that, they were related to the unicorn's legendary powers. In her book *The Unicorn Alphabet* (lavishly illustrated by Michael Hague), Marianna Mayer explains the curative characteristics of the plants pictured in the famous tapestries and their links to the unicorn.

> For instance, during the Renaissance period French people considered the columbine a symbol of loyalty—a quality also associated with the unicorn. Moreover, the lovely flower was believed to protect against poison, as was the unicorn's horn. Irises and marigolds were said to cure snakebites, and as folklore tells us, the unicorn's horn neutralized the venom of poisonous serpents who polluted the waters of the world. In those days, people planted violets in their gardens to safeguard against evil, and of course, the unicorn is well known as a champion against evil of all kinds.

The scene shows us that the unicorn has given up his freedom for love, for he could certainly escape the modest enclosure if he wanted to. But it also symbolizes the risen Christ—one of the major metaphors associated with the unicorn—for the animal that was previously slain by the hunters (as chronicled in the earlier tapestries) now appears alive and well, risen from certain death with no sign of the wounds the hunters inflicted upon it.

The Unicorn Tapestries in Movies

The Unicorn in Captivity tapestry shows up in several places in the movie *Harry Potter and the Half-Blood Prince*. An image of the fountain in the second panel, *The Unicorn Is Found*, appears in the opening scenes of *The Last Unicorn*.

Six more famous unicorn tapestries, collectively known as *The Lady and the Unicorn* series or the *Cluny Tapestries*, hang in the Musée National du Moyen Âge in Paris (formerly the Musée de Cluny). Believed to have been woven at the same time and place as the seven panels in *The Hunt for the Unicorn* series, they are equally elaborate and elegant, with vibrant colors and *mille-fleurs* (thousand flowers) backgrounds. Each depicts a noblewoman with a unicorn and a lion, and sometimes other animals or birds.

Five tapestries in the series represent the five senses: sight, hearing, taste, smell, and touch. In the panel *Sight*, the lady holds a mirror, while the unicorn lays its head in her lap and gazes at its reflection—after all, it's only natural that such a beautiful beast would want to admire its comely countenance. In *Hearing*, the noblewoman plays an organ while the unicorn and the lion hold up banners. In addition to the unicorn and the lion, a monkey appears in the panel *Taste* eating sweets fed to it by the lady. The lady crafts a floral wreath in *Smell* while her lady-in-waiting hands her fresh flowers. In *Touch* the lady shows her preference for the unicorn by laying her hand on its horn, while the lion sits off to the side.

Some sources say the sixth tapestry, titled *À mon seul désir* (my sole desire), signifies love, for at this time the idealized concept of courtly love still flourished among the noble classes of Europe and Britain. (See Chapter 1 for more information.) However, it's also possible that the panel refers to a desire for lasting peace between the warring nations of England and Scotland, symbolized by the unicorn (Scotland) and the lion (England).

Rescuing the Tapestries

When *The Lady and the Unicorn* tapestries were discovered in 1841 in the Boussac castle in central France, they had been damaged by damp conditions and had mildewed badly. The noted French writer George Sand championed their salvation in her novel *Jeanne*. Sand's knowledge of women's period clothing enabled her to correctly date the time when the tapestries were woven.

CHASTITY AND THE UNICORN

During the Renaissance, chastity was highly valued in women—especially those of noble birth. Among high-born women, virginity was a requirement for marriage. In this intensely religious period, the Christian church emphasized the virginity of Mary the Mother of Christ, expecting human women to follow in Mary's footsteps.

But there were practical reasons for encouraging chastity as well. For instance, there was the ever-present problem of venereal disease, for which no cure existed at the time. Additionally, in societies where nobles and royalty needed to be certain of their lineage and offspring—entire kingdoms rested upon knowing who'd spawned whom—aristocratic wives had to maintain their fidelity. Not only their social station, but their very lives depended on it.

As Sharan Newman, author of *Guinevere* (the first book in her Guinevere trilogy), points out in a 1999 interview with Raymond H. Thompson for the University of Rochester's Camelot Project, people in those days placed great importance on sense of duty. "There was a desperate need to keep the old social order going and to maintain your place in it; to keep up the mask as long as you could, because otherwise chaos would prevail."

Unicorn-Drawn Chariots

Petrarch (Francesco Petrarca), the great fourteenth-century lyric poet and philosopher, penned a collection of poems known as the *Trionfi* that addresses the subjects of love, chastity, death, fame, time, and eternity. In it, he describes a "triumphal car" that the illustrators of his book rendered as a chariot called "The Triumph of Chastity," drawn by unicorns, sometimes as many as six. The unicorns appear with the usual equine bodies, cloven hooves, and curlicue horns. Petrarch's *Trionfi* was so popular during the Renaissance that it was translated into all the major European languages of the time.

A Symbol of Chastity in Art

Marriage portraits, which gained popularity during the Renaissance, often included symbols that signified the lady's chastity. Considering that pretty much everybody was familiar with the lovely white unicorn's reputation for purity and nobility—and the legend that only a virgin could tame a unicorn—it's no surprise that Renaissance artists often featured the animal in their paintings of women. Of course, the unicorn is also an obvious symbol of masculinity with that unabashedly phallic horn. The idea that he surrenders to a virgin represented the lady's ability to resist sexual temptation.

In the marriage portraits painted by Maestro delle Storie del Pane, *Portrait of a Man* and *Portrait of a Woman* (circa 1485–1495), a unicorn appears in the background of the bride's portrait to indicate her virginity. Then there's Raphael's well-known oil painting *Young Woman with Unicorn* (circa 1506). In it, the woman holds a diminutive unicorn perched directly on her lap—you can't get more blatant than that.

Young Woman with Unicorn
by Raffaello Sanzio da Urbino, 1506

Unicorn or Lap Dog?

X-rays and other modern investigative techniques now let experts peek below the surface layers of oil and pigment to see how the Old Masters went about developing their paintings. What lies beneath the unicorn in Raphael's picture? A lap dog. Art historians think that in the original painting, the lady's hands were probably empty and that later artists added the dog, then finally the unicorn to suggest her chastity.

The Unicorn as a Symbol of Sexuality

Despite the unicorn's connection with purity and chastity, its sexual imagery couldn't be more obvious—the creature's most notable feature, after all, is its distinctly phallic horn. The American writer, professor, and politician, Odell Shepard in his 1930 book *The Lore of the Unicorn* describes a different view of the maiden and the unicorn: " . . . they lead forth a young virgin, pure and chaste, to whom, when the animal sees her, he approaches, throwing himself upon her. Then the girl offers him her breasts, and the animal begins to suck the breasts of the maiden and to conduct himself familiarly with her."

In *Gargantua and Pantagruel*, the French Renaissance physician, writer, and scholar, François Rabelais, described the unicorn's anatomy more suggestively. He proposed that ordinarily, the horn hung limp, "like a turkey-cock's comb. When an unicorn has a mind to fight or put it to some other use, what does it do but make it stand, and then 'tis straight as an arrow."

A similar description, taken from *The South African Christian Reporter* and recounted in the 1886 book *Mythological Monsters*, claims that in southern Africa lives "a horse, extremely fleet and strong, with a single horn from two feet to two and a half feet in length, projecting from its forehead, which is said to be flexible when the animal is asleep, and capable of being curled up at pleasure, but becoming stiff and hard under the excitement of rage. It is extremely fierce, and invariably attacks a man when it discerns him."

"The unicorn stands alone, still as frost. It keeps watch down the corridors of time. The past and the future meet in the presence of the unicorn; the darkness and light become one. Patient as a candle flame, inviolate, here is our guardian, keeper of the silent unknown."

—Josephine Bradley, *In Pursuit of the Unicorn*

WILL THE REAL VIRGIN PLEASE STAND UP?

The term "virginity" connotes more than a lack of sexual intercourse, as Theodore Sturgeon conveys in his beautifully written story "The Silken-Swift." In this 1953 tale, Sturgeon presents a provocative tale of a privileged and beautiful temptress named Rita who, although technically a virgin, entices and toys with the affections of a young man named Del. After an evening with the teasing Rita, young Del, deluded, angry, and half-crazed with desire, rapes a simple, kindhearted woman named Barbara who admires him and wants to take care of him. But Barbara isn't a hapless victim—she has a powerful and magical ally: a unicorn that comes to drink at the pond near where she lives.

A skeptical Del challenges Rita's claim of virginity, and they agree that the unicorn will decide—for as everyone knows, unicorns can detect a virgin from the length of a football field. But when put to the test, the unicorn shuns Rita and lays its head in Barbara's lap instead. The story's moral is that "purity" is a matter of heart and mind, not body—and the wise unicorn can instantly spot those who are pure of heart, regardless of physical technicalities.

Diana Peterfreund, author of the Killer Unicorns series, tackles the issue from another perspective in her 2010 book *Ascendant*. In Peterfreund's books, which feature girl unicorn hunters, only a virgin can kill the dangerous unicorns. She raises the question of what virginity really means by introducing "the lesbian loophole." Is a woman who has never had sexual intercourse with a man, but enjoys female sex partners, exempt from the technical definition and therefore able to hunt unicorns successfully? In an interview with fellow writer Malinda Lo, Peterfreund discusses patriarchal society's definition of virginity and what constitutes "real" sex. Says Peterfreund, "My hope is that placing these questions in a fantasy scenario helps to foster conversations."

> "For the creature requires not that she has never known the touch of men, only that an untempored longing for that touch has not closed her inner vision . . ."

—Michael Green, *De Historia et Veritate Unicornis*

THE LION AND THE UNICORN

During the late Middle Ages and the Renaissance, coats of arms that featured mythical creatures and symbolic elements gained popularity. Although unicorn emblems appeared on seals and coins all the way back in ancient Babylonia and Assyria, Scotland's James III popularized them in the 1400s. Clans, as well as towns and even countries, adopted these richly emblematic designs, which medieval soldiers originally had displayed in battle to let everyone know which side they were fighting for.

Symbols of Scotland and England

In heraldry, the unicorn represents Scotland—the monarch's coat of arms for the Kingdom of Scotland featured two unicorns supporting a central shield. The unicorn became part of the royal shield of Scotland in the 1300s, after a long and bloody war that resulted in Scotland gaining independence from England. Because his countrymen were familiar with the animal's strength, purity, and valor, King Robert III chose the unicorn as a symbol to inspire his people as they rebuilt their nation.

In 1603, when King James VI of Scotland inherited the English throne and became King James I of both England and Scotland, he revised the crest. The new royal coat of arms depicted both the Scottish unicorn and the lion of England, symbolizing the reunion of the two countries (they were formally joined by the Acts of Union a century later in 1707).

Although both Scotland and England's coats of arms include the unicorn and the lion, some differences prevail. The English version, for example, pictures the lion wearing a crown on its head. In the Scottish version, the unicorn also wears a crown.

Unicorn Coins

In the fifteenth century, Scotland's monetary system included two gold coins known as the unicorn and the half-unicorn. Both coins were engraved with the image of the unicorn.

The Lion and the Unicorn in Myth

The symbolism incorporated into the United Kingdom's coat of arms is particularly interesting because it harkens back to early myths that describe the lion and the unicorn as enemies:

- The ancient Greeks spoke of unicorns battling lions.
- Middle Eastern lore describes the lion and the unicorn in astrological terms—two beings that have engaged in an intricate dance since the beginning of time. For fourteen years, it's said, the lion chases the unicorn across the sky. Then they reverse roles and the unicorn chases the lion for fourteen years.

- Ancient Babylonian legends equate the unicorn with spring and the lion with summer. Each year the two fight, but the lion always overtakes the unicorn.
- Other myths connect the lion with the sun and the unicorn with the moon: opposites and complements.
- In Japanese and Korean mythology, the unicorn was considered the regent of the land, rivaling the lion as king of beasts in the West.

Perhaps the symbolism stems from the fact that in Africa lions prey upon animals such as the oryx and the eland, animals that provide possible prototypes for unicorns. But these antelopes aren't helpless victims—they fight back and can spear the lions with their horns.

"The Lion-sun flies from the rising Unicorn-moon and hides behind the Tree or Grove of the Underworld; The Moon pursues, and, sinking in Her turn, is sun slain."

—Robert Brown, *The Unicorn: A Mythological Investigation* (1881)

Kevin Owens, writing on the website All about Unicorns, suggests that the "Lion represents the urge to impose one's idea of order upon the world, while the Unicorn exemplifies the drive to bring harmony through insight and understanding. Their effects are often identical, but their different approaches tend to promote strife. However, when the Lion and the Unicorn work in harmony toward the same goal, no other creature can withstand them because they represent a union of opposites."

James Huneker, in his book *Unicorns*, tells us that the crown for which the two beasts fight symbolizes art, and the struggle represents the conflict between the rational mind and the imagination. "The crown is Art, and the Lion, being a realist born, is only attracted by its glitter, not the symbol. The Unicorn, an idealist, divines the inner meaning of this precious fillet of gold. Art is the modern philosopher's stone, and the most brilliant jewel in this much-contested crown."

Unicorn Armor

In the late fifteenth century, European cavalrymen began outfitting their war horses with a type of head gear on which a spike was affixed. The spike thus protruded from the animal's forehead. Known as a "panache," the harness allowed the horse to perform as a weapon as well as a soldier's mount.

Trapping the Unicorn Through Trickery

The animosity between the unicorn and the lion is expressed in another legend, which may have its roots in a twelfth-century letter that supposedly originated in an Ethiopian king's court. The "letter" explains that the savvy lion uses a clever trick to capture a unicorn. The lion stands in front of a large tree and taunts his enemy until the unicorn charges, horn positioned to gore the lion. But at the last moment, the lion jumps away and the unicorn impales the tree, trapping itself. Naturally, the lion feasts on its prey.

Unicorns and Trees

In legends, unicorns and trees have another commonality too. Both, if not actually immortal, live for a very long time. The giant redwoods of the Pacific Northwest, for instance, can live up to 2,000 years, and some ancient pine trees in California's Inyo National Forest are said to be nearly 5,000 years old. A 4,000-year-old cypress called the Zoroastrian Sarv is an Iranian national monument and believed to be one of the oldest living things in all of Asia. Yew trees are also famous for their longevity—the Llangernyw Yew in a northern Wales churchyard is estimated to be 4,000 years old. Some sources also suggest that the curling ribs on the unicorn's horn, like tree rings, signify periods of time. The longer and more twisted the horn, the older (and wiser) the unicorn.

"Like as a Lion whose imperial power
A proud rebellious Unicorn defies,
T'avoid the rash assault and wrathful stout
Of his fierce foe, him to a tree applies,
And when him running in full course he spies,
He slips aside; the whiles that furious beast
His precious horn, sought of his enemies,
Strikes in the stock, nor thence can be released,
But to the mighty victor yields a bounteous feast."

—Edmund Spenser, *The Faerie Queene* (1590–1596)

In *Julius Caesar*, Shakespeare refers to the legendary lion's ruse when Decius says of Caesar (who was linked symbolically with the lion), "He loves to hear that unicorns may be betray'd with trees." In the fairy tale "The Valiant Little Tailor" from the Brothers Grimm, a tailor tricks a unicorn in the same way by standing in front of a tree himself and enticing the beast to charge (see Chapter 8).

Wood for Wands

Wizards, witches, and other magical practitioners have long prized the wood of the yew tree for making magic wands, perhaps because of the yew's long lifespan. In the Harry Potter stories, the evil Lord Voldemort's wand was made of yew.

The Lion and the Unicorn in Contemporary Literature

Lewis Carroll, a.k.a. Charles Dodgson, includes a lion and a unicorn as characters in his book *Through the Looking-Glass and What Alice Found There* (published 1871). Although it's not clear whether he intended the two adversarial creatures to represent the British Parliament's contrary factions—William Gladstone of the Liberals and Benjamin Disraeli, leader of the Conservative Party— the animals amuse us nonetheless with their foolishness.

The lion and the unicorn serve as political symbols in the works of many other writers, including George Orwell ("The Lion and the Unicorn: Socialism and the English Genius"), Richard Aldous (*The*

Lion and the Unicorn: Gladstone vs. Disraeli), and Sir Arthur Bryant (*The Lion and the Unicorn: A Personal History of Twentieth-Century England*).

In Neil Gaiman's novel *Stardust*, the protagonist Tristran Thorn and a fallen star named Yvaine observe a lion and a unicorn battling over a golden crown. Just as the lion is about to slay the unicorn, Tristran Thorn recalls an old nursery rhyme that describes the struggles between England and Scotland. He grabs the crown and gives it to the lion, who seems satisfied with his prize and retreats back into the forest. The unicorn survives.

> "The lion and the unicorn
> Were fighting for the crown;
> The lion beat the unicorn
> All round about the town.
> Some gave them white bread
> And some gave them brown;
> Some gave them plum cake
> And drummed them out of town."

—English nursery rhyme

The rhyme shows up again in the last episode of *Batman: The Animated Series* "The Lion and the Unicorn" (1995). Here, the character Alfred Pennyworth recites the rhyme, which turns out to contain a secret code.

The Chronicles of Narnia, by C.S. Lewis, however, turns the tables on the age-old animosity between the unicorn and the lion. In these tales, the magnificent unicorn Jewel is the loyal and devoted friend of the lion Aslan, the one true king of the land of Narnia (see Chapter 9 for more).

UNICORN SIGHTING

The German Jesuit missionary and mathematics professor, Johann Greuber, traveled to China in 1656 and wrote about seeing a number of unfamiliar animals there. "Sining [Xining, the capital of Qinghai province] is a great and populous city, built at the vast wall of China, through the gate of which the merchants from India enter Katay or China. There are stairs to go a-top of the wall, and many travel on it from the gate at Sining to the next at Soochew, which is eighteen days' journey, having a delightful prospect all the way, from the wall, of the innumerable habitations on one side, and the various wild beasts which range the desert on the other side. Besides wild bulls, here are tigers, lions, elephants, rhinoceroses, and monoceroses, which are a kind of horned asses. Thus the merchants view the beasts free from danger."

THE ALICON EXPOSED

Well into the Renaissance and beyond, people still believed in the purifying powers of the unicorn's horn, or alicon as it was called, and continued to pay exorbitant prices to obtain its highly touted medicinal benefits. So widespread was the assumption of the magical horn's curative abilities that apothecaries latched onto the unicorn as their "logo." Often they featured the animal on their signs or displayed the "horn" in their shop windows. Because the narwhal's tusk is ivory—as many people believed the unicorn's horn to be made of— early "tests" confirmed its validity and perpetuated the legend.

A Protected Unicorn

A UNESCO World Heritage Site at Pilsen in the Czech Republic presents a handsome example of the unicorn as a symbol of Renaissance apothecaries. The three-dimensional head of a white unicorn protrudes from a golden cornice above the doorway of "The White Unicorn" pharmacy, inviting passersby to come in and purchase cures for their ills.

But after European explorers began traveling to the Arctic regions, where they sighted the actual source of the "alicon"— namely, the narwhal—the ruse was up. In the mid-sixteenth century, the Swedish writer Olaus Magnus drew the earliest map of the Nordic countries, known as the Carta Marina. On it he depicted a strange "sea unicorn," bearing a long, spiral-shaped tusk and swimming in the waters off Scandinavia. In 1638, Danish zoologist Ole Worm identified the creature as the alicon's true owner. It turned out that even an alicon belonging to England's Queen Elizabeth I was really a narwhal's tusk, brought back from Labrador by the noted British seaman Martin Frobisher in 1577.

The Curative Properties of Rhino Horns

Over the centuries, rhino horns had often been substituted for those of the fabled unicorn and proclaimed to have amazing healing properties. When Pope Gregory XIV lay on his deathbed in 1590, the Prior and the Brothers of the Monastery of Saint Mary in Guadalupe, Spain presented him with a legendary cure: the horn of an African white rhinoceros, but to no avail. The pope died shortly thereafter.

One of the finest "unicorn" horns belonged to Pope Clement VII. The pope commissioned the noted sixteenth-century Italian artist Benvenuto Cellini to sculpt a base for it. Cellini, in his autobiography, writes, "I had designed the finest head imaginable; for I took it partly from the horse and partly from the stag, enriching it with fantastic mane and other ornaments." Of course, the horn turned out to be a narwhal's tusk.

Once the forgeries were revealed, the church began distancing itself from the unicorn. The Council of Trent in 1563 ruled against using the unicorn as a symbol for Christ any longer. In art and literature, the unicorn would hence be treated as a mythological creature instead of a spiritual one, representing romantic love but not divine love.

UNICORN SIGHTING

In his 1886 book *Mythological Monsters*, Charles Gould recounts the experience of the Roman adventurer Lewes Vertomannus, who traveled to Egypt and Arabia in 1503. Vertomannus visited "the Temple of Mecha" where he saw unicorns "which are not seen in any other place . . .

"On the other part of the temple are parks or places enclosed, where are seen two unicorns, named of the Greeks monocerotse, and are there showed to the people for a miracle, and not without good reason, for the seldomness and strange nature . . . This beast doubtless seemeth wild and fierce, yet tempereth that fierceness with a certain comeliness. These unicorns one gave to the Sultan of Mecha as a most precious and rare gift. They were sent him out of Ethiope by a king of that country who desired by that present to gratify the Sultan of Mecha."

RENAISSANCE UNICORNS TODAY

Where's the best place to spot a unicorn today? Why, at a Renaissance Faire, of course. Each year, hundreds of thousands of people visit this colorful period at sites across the United States, as well as Canada, the United Kingdom, Europe, and Australia. Some locales feature permanent "settlements" where you can see jousting knights, kings and queens, wandering minstrels, jesters, jugglers, acrobats, and exotic animals—including unicorns.

Started in 1963, the Original Renaissance Pleasure Faire of Southern California is the oldest in the United States. Held in April and May in Irwindale, California, it boasts more than 200,000 attendees annually. Faires seek to reproduce villages, marketplaces, royal courts, and other period places in an entertaining way—without the plague and pestilence. *Renaissance Magazine*'s website *www.renaissancemagazine.com/fairelist.html* provides a list of Faires in and outside of the United States where you can partake of the fun. You might even get to ride (or at least pat) a unicorn!

CHAPTER 7

Unicorns in the Age of Enlightenment: Science Confronts Mythology

"The unicorn legend is different from most superstitions in that it has lasted longer and has been shared by the most enlightened minds of all nations."

—Andrea Bacci, Italian botanist, zoologist, and physician

AFTER A THOUSAND years during which mysticism, religious piety, and fascination with the supernatural held sway in Europe and elsewhere, a "prove it to me" backlash ushered in the so-called Age of Enlightenment in the seventeenth and eighteenth centuries. Its proponents urged a critical, "scientific" approach to ideas of a social, philosophical, and particularly a religious nature, and they sought to discredit anything that didn't hold up to the rigid rules of reason and logic. If you couldn't touch, see, hear, smell, or taste something—or preferably, measure and weigh it and analyze its chemical composition—it wasn't "real." The materialistic ideas of that period have trickled down through the centuries and still influence our attitudes today.

So where does this leave the unicorn? At the time, the general populace believed unicorns did, indeed, exist, even if they'd never actually seen the magical creature or dragged home its bones, cloven hooves, or spiral-shaped horn as proof. But skeptics now challenged the public's faith in the creature's validity. Never mind that the unicorn had abided for eons in the minds of human beings around the world—anyone who clung to the old myths risked ridicule. Evidence that the "unicorn horns" purveyed by apothecaries throughout the Middle Ages and the Renaissance for healing purposes turned out to be tusks from narwhals, rhinos, and other ordinary creatures, supported the skeptics' claims.

> ## "God himself must needs be traduced, if there is no unicorn in the world."
>
> —Edward Topsell, in his 1607 Bestiary

Unicorns, however, never put themselves out there to be examined by scientists, for they are above the business of proving themselves to skeptics. This makes it extremely difficult for people who need to quantify, qualify, and examine tangible evidence of unicorns in order to believe in them.

UNICORNS IN THE NEW WORLD

till, some people in the scientific and educated communities entertained the possibility that the unicorn was alive and well, perhaps in the wild and as yet uncharted New World. In 1673, a Dutch doctor named Olfert Dapper proposed in his illustrated book *Die unbekannte Neue Welt* that unicorns could be found in New Amsterdam (New York City), maybe grazing contentedly in what's now the Bronx. Even more intriguing, Dr. Dapper's book pictures the unicorn with an American eagle perched on its back.

His text, however, places the creature's habitat closer to upstate New York. "On the Canadian border there are sometimes seen animals resembling horses, but with cloven hoofs, rough manes, a long straight horn upon the forehead, a curled tail like that of the wild boar, black eyes, and a neck like that of the stag. They live in the loneliest wildernesses and are so shy that the males do not even pasture with the females except in the season of rut, when they are not so wild. As soon as this season is past, however, they fight not only with other beasts but even with those of their own kind."

A century earlier, the British naval commander Sir John Hawkins had sailed to Florida, where he encountered natives with "pieces of unicornes hornes which they wear about their necks, whereof the Frenchmen obtained many pieces. Of those unicornes they have many; for that they doe affirme it to be a beast with one horne, which comming to the river to drinke, putteth the same into the water before he drinketh. Of this unicornes horne there are of our company, that having gotten the same of the Frenchmen, brought horne thereof to shew . . . It is thought that there are lions and tygres as well as unicornes; lions especially; if it be true that is sayd, of the enmity betweene them and the unicornes: for there is no beast but hath his enemy insomuch that whereas the one is the other cannot be missing."

UNICORN SIGHTING

In April 2013, a hiker in Pennsylvania's Tiadaghton State Forest stumbled upon a cave that held an amazing find: the skull of an animal with a single horn extending from its forehead. The skull lay in a wooden box, along with some beads, broken bits of a clay pot, and what might have been a rusted metal blade. The following month, researchers at the *Journal of the Bizarre* examined the unusual skull and determined it once belonged to a male deer or similar creature. They estimated the animal may have lived in the seventeenth century, and that the Andaste tribe might have used the skull as part of a ritual. Could this be an example of the unicorn Dr. Dapper wrote about?

THE CONFLICT BETWEEN RATIONALISM AND MYSTICISM

During the eighteenth and nineteenth centuries, science and religion found themselves on opposite ends of the playing field. Writers and philosophers, such as the American political activist Thomas Paine (1736–1809), began challenging the authority and legitimacy of the Bible, the Christian Church, and religion in general. In both England and the United States, members of the intelligentsia embraced a movement away from mysticism and toward a more analytical, scientific approach to understanding the universe. Fueled by a series of wars between Catholic France and Protestant England (1793–1815), people on both sides of the Atlantic questioned the religious and mythical ideas that had predominated until now.

In the wave of contention and controversy, pretty much anything of a mystical nature was subject to criticism. Unicorns, in particular, had a long-standing connection with Christian mythology, as we've already discussed in earlier chapters. The educated, free-thinking, "enlightened" folks in this period contested Christianity's view of the universe and looked down on Old World superstition, including unicorns, as the stuff only illiterate peasants would believe in—and they considered themselves well above all that. As a result, unicorns, along with mermaids, dragons, fairies, and other fantastic, inexplicable beings became as passé as last year's shoes.

Scientific Arguments Against the Unicorn

Researchers such as the French naturalist Baron Georges Léopold Cuvier (1769–1832) analyzed fossils of long-gone beasts, in an attempt to comprehend our distant past. As a result of his studies, Cuvier proposed that it was impossible for a unicorn to sprout a single horn in the vicinity of its mystical "third eye" because the horn couldn't grow over a bone division present in the creature's forehead.

UNICORN SIGHTING

Sir Thomas Browne, in his *Pseudodoxia Epidemica: or, Enquiries into Very Many Received Tenets and Commonly Presumed Truths* (1646, 1672), stated, "[W]e are so far from denying there is any Unicorn at all, that we affirm there are many kinds thereof. In the number of Quadrupedes, we will concede no less then five; that is, the Indian Ox, the Indian Ass, the Rhinoceros, the Oryx, and that which is more eminently termed Monoceros, or Unicornis. Some in the list of fishes; as that described by Olaus, Albertus and others: and some Unicorns we will allow even among Insects; as those four kinds of nasicornous Beetles described by Muffetus."

Where's the Proof?

Although people could still purchase ground unicorn horn in apothecaries as late as the mid-eighteenth century, tests had shown conclusively that the substance actually came from the tusks of other creatures—and even the bones of domestic animals and humans. Physicians doubted the possibility that any single medicine could remedy every illness known to humankind, as was claimed by the proponents of the unicorn horn who touted it as a magical cure-all. For centuries, both serious researchers and curiosity seekers had been searching the world for evidence of the elusive unicorn, yet no one had found anything that could stand up to scientific scrutiny. Faith in the beloved, mystical creature's physical existence was dwindling, at least among the scientific community.

Still Precious after All These Years

Christie's in London knew the "unicorn's horn" it put up for auction in 1994 came from a narwhal, not the fabled unicorn, but the twelfth-century tusk still fetched almost half a million pounds. Elaborately carved with the images of dragons and other mythical creatures, it had been housed in Hereford Cathedral Close in Hereford, England, perhaps for centuries, until it was sold in 1957 as a walking stick for twelve pounds.

Nigel Suckling, in his 2007 book *Unicorns*, recounts the reaction of David Ekserdjian, then head of Christie's sculpture department, to the treasure: "It was wrapped up in a newspaper inside a cardboard tube, but the minute I held it in my hand I knew I was in the presence of a great and extraordinary object. There was something about its weight and heft, as well as the sheer beauty of its carving. It has an almost tangible power, something you can feel coursing through your veins."

Terrestrial and Aquatic Unicorns

Despite the skepticism that arose when unicorn horns were exposed as hoaxes, many people continued to believe that unicorns existed. In those days, as Chris Lavers explains in *The Natural History of Unicorns*, "it was widely believed that all terrestrial animals had marine counterparts. If unicorns existed in the sea, it stood to reason that they also existed on land." So, in a way, knowledge of the narwhal actually reinforced rather than diminished the assumption among the general public that the unicorn was real.

One noted thinker of the time, the eighteenth-century German philosopher Immanuel Kant, took issue with the idea that material proof was necessary for something to be considered "real." He pointed out that no one has yet provided physical evidence of God, but that doesn't mean God doesn't exist—nor does a lack of proof stop people from believing in Him. According to Kant, material existence doesn't make an entity more real. His argument could apply to unicorns too.

Unicorns in the Sky

In 1624, the German mathematician Jacob Bartsch depicted a constellation named Monoceros the Unicorn on his star charts. The constellation contains 146 stars visible to the naked eye, including two "blue giant" stars—known together as Plasketts' Star—with a total mass of about one hundred times that of our own sun. Located at the celestial equator, Monoceros intersects with the Milky Way. In 1690, astronomer Johannes Hevelius (who built an observatory at Danzig, Poland) wrote about the constellation in his volume *Johannes Hevelius and His Catalog of the Stars*.

THE UNICORN ACCORDING TO GUERICKE AND LEIBNIZ

While all this pooh-poohing was going on, two German scientists took an interest in the unicorn after unidentified prehistoric bones were discovered in Germany's *Einhornhöhle* (translation: unicorn cave) in 1663. Otto von Guericke, Mayor of Magdeburg for thirty-one years, wasn't just a politician, he was also a respected philosopher, scientist, and inventor. Europe's scientific community liked him.

"It happened in the year 1663 in Quedlinburg [about halfway between Hamburg and Dresden], that on the Mountain the common people call Zeunickenberg, where lime is mined, inside the rock a unicorn skeleton was found," von Guericke recounted. "The rear portion of the body, as is common in a beast, lay back, head up, but, extending lengthwise from the brow was a horn, the thickness of a human leg, and so in proportion to the length of almost five cubits."

After the bones were brought out of the cave, von Guericke had them assembled to form an oddity that he claimed was the skeleton of a unicorn. Perhaps the ugliest monstrosity ever to bear the label "unicorn," the composite creature had only two front legs and the skull of a woolly rhinoceros. Its vertebrae once belonged to a mammoth, and most likely its horn was a mammoth tusk or perhaps that of a palaeoloxodon, a type of elephant that became extinct 15,000 years prior to the mammoth. The peculiar beast's remains took up residence near the zoo at Osnabrück.

About thirty years later, Gottfried Wilhelm von Leibniz, a mathematician credited with the development of calculus, was working with fossils in connection with his geological history of north-central Germany. He sketched the unicorn-curiosity, and in 1749, more than thirty years after Leibniz's death, Ludwig Scheidt, the librarian of the House of Brunswick, collected the drawings and had them published in Latin and German as *Protogaea, or A Dissertation on the Original Aspect of the Earth and the Vestiges of Its Very Ancient History in the Monuments of Nature.* Early in the nineteenth century, the Austrian paleontologist Othenio Abel mentioned the sketches in his books. Clearly, these scientists believed that the unicorn had existed—if not in the present, at least in the past—despite contradictory reports from skeptical sources.

Today, if you visit the *Einhornhöhle* you'll see a life-size replica of the creature's skeleton standing in front of the cave. Museums in the area exhibit its "bones." You can even bring its picture home with you on a T-shirt or coffee mug.

Before the seventeenth century, the word "fossil" meant pretty much any old thing you dug up from the ground. Later, the term became associated with petrified, organic material. Ivory—from the tusks of ancient mammoths, rhinos, or other species—was dubbed *unicornu fossili* or "unicorn fossil."

"Perhaps it is simply a matter of faith or perhaps those ancient noblemen of Brocileande were on the right track. Maybe the trick is to instill in the Unicorn a wish to seek out the human who wants to gaze upon it with his or her very own eyes. Unicorns are empathic and sensitive to the desire in an individual. Unicorns are able to judge if that person is true to their heart, if they are to be trusted . . . if they will prove to be a true friend. Nothing is certain, but maybe if a person believes the Unicorn is actually there . . . who knows?"

—The Guardhouse: "Britannica The Unicorn,"
www.novareinna.com/guard/unicorn.html

After the end of the Age of Enlightenment, during which reason and scientific analysis held sway, the pendulum swung back, ushering in the Romantic Era. As you might suspect, the unicorn came along with it.

UNICORN SIGHTING

The Swedish naturalist, Dr. Anders Sparrman, traveled to the Cape of Good Hope in the late eighteenth century in search of the fabled unicorn. In his "Travels," (a journal he kept; recounted by V.S. Forbes and published in 1977 by the Van Riebeeck Society in Cape Town, South Africa) he wrote that the African tribe known as the Hottentots told him about a rare and very swift horse-like animal with a single horn on its forehead. The tribe killed one of the animals, which was described as resembling a horse, gray with white stripes, with a single pointed horn that was attached only to the skin at the creature's forehead.

CHAPTER 8

Romancing the Unicorn: The Romantic and Victorian Eras

"In the midnight forest the dark oak trees are still under the stars. The pale wildflowers in the clearing have furled their petals for the night. Suddenly he appears, a milk-white creature with the proud form of a horse. You may not notice his cloven hoofs or curling beard, but you see the curved neck, the silver mane, the graceful tail. Then he moves his head, and the moonlight runs like sea water along the pearly spiral of his horn. There is no sound, but at the next heart-beat the clearing is once again empty of all but the night."

—Georgess McHargue, *The Beasts of Never*

THE AGE OF ENLIGHTENMENT pretty much squelched serious discussion of the unicorn as a flesh-and-blood animal— at least among the intelligentsia—but the hope that such a creature might exist never really died. Yes, the church had distanced itself from the unicorn as a metaphor for Christ, and science had revealed that the celebrated unicorn's magic healing horn was a fake. But the creature's connection with purity, romantic love, and beauty remained in the hearts and minds of the people who still loved the unicorn.

During the Romantic Era, beauty was considered reason enough for something to prevail—and few things could match the beauty of the unicorn. Paul and Karin Johnsgard, in their book *Dragons and Unicorns: A Natural History*, explain, "As the symbolic significance of the unicorn dwindled in the Church, it grew in Romantic literature. There the unicorn became associated with gentle and romantic love and with spiritual purity. Thus, it was the Romantics who ultimately saved the unicorn from complete extinction, by raising the creature above the level of religious allegory and medical quackery to that of simple beauty. No longer linked with treachery, pain, and death, the unicorn was finally set free to roam the vistas of the mind, with beauty its only excuse for existing..."

In the late eighteenth century, another wave of adventurers, entrepreneurs, missionaries, and anthropologists expanded their range of investigation into the earth's uncharted regions. Interest in the unicorn swelled, as explorers began traveling to parts of Asia, the Himalayas, Africa, and other distant regions of the earth in search of it. If they could find and capture the legendary beast of poetry and mysticism, what incredible fame and fortune might they reap?

UNICORN SIGHTING

The Scottish Christian missionary John Campbell in his *Travels in South Africa* (published in 1815) describes an animal killed by the African tribe known as the Hottentots. According to Campbell, "the head they brought us had a straight horn projecting three feet from the forehead, about ten inches above the tip of the nose. The projection of this great horn very much resembles that of the fanciful unicorn in the British [coat of] arms."

EMBRACING FANTASY AND THE SUPERNATURAL

uring the Romantic Era, which lasted from about 1780 until 1850, artists, poets, musicians, and other creative individuals reacted to the science-dominated Age of Enlightenment. The pendulum swung back once again. Now emotion, imagination, fantasy, and the supernatural enjoyed a revival. Themes of dark and light, demons and angels, villains and heroes thrived, often entwined with mysticism and sentimentality.

Many of our contemporary fantasy films, including those by the great directors George Lucas and Steven Spielberg, can trace their artistic roots to this period. Novels of the time served as precursors to today's popular fiction genres, including horror, gothic, fantasy, and sci-fi. Mary Shelley published her immortal novel *Frankenstein* in 1818. John Polidori's *The Vampyre* followed a year later. Although Bram Stoker's *Dracula* didn't come into print until 1897, vampires had already established themselves as subjects in European literature by the mid-1700s.

The Unicorn and the Vampire

In Sarah Beth Durst's 2011 novel *Drink, Slay, Love*, a unicorn spears a teenage vampire named Pearl with his horn. The infusion of goodness injected by the unicorn's purifying horn gives the vampire-girl a conscience—a modern take on the ancient idea that the unicorn's horn can nullify poison, cure illness, and recognize evil. Now Pearl starts questioning some of the practices she previously accepted—such as leading her friends like lambs to the slaughter.

What sparked the interest in supernatural beings during the eighteenth and nineteenth centuries? A backlash against the materialism of the Age of Reason, as we've already discussed, was only partly responsible. This was also the time of the Industrial Revolution in Europe and the United States, during which people feared that machines were usurping humanity. Science and technology took away some of the mystery that had previously engaged our ancestors' minds.

Many Europeans and Americans began rejecting traditional religions, or had already done so during the Age of Reason. Now they turned to Spiritualism, mysticism, and occultism. Noted writers, among them Sir Arthur Conan Doyle (creator of the Sherlock

Holmes series) and poet Elizabeth Barrett Browning, embraced paranormal ideas. Even Britain's Queen Victoria and Prince Albert attended séances during the mid-1800s. A widespread belief in an invisible world and things that science couldn't explain opened the doors for all sorts of fantastic possibilities, including unicorns.

THE ADVENT OF FAIRY TALES FOR CHILDREN

ew developments in literature for children during the Romantic and Victorian Eras brought the unicorn into the spotlight once again. Previously, books written for children emphasized education and moral training, in preparation for adulthood. Now, they endeavored to delight young audiences as well.

Books and story collections, such as *Children's and Household Tales* by Jacob and Wilhelm Grimm and *The Thousand and One Nights*, appeared in the 1800s. The popularity of these books inspired other authors in Europe and America, including Hans Christian Andersen and Nathaniel Hawthorne, ushering in a tradition of fairy tales and folk stories for young people that would continue into the present day.

Childhood Innocence

Romantic writers depicted children as pure, innocent beings—a "blank slate" or *tabula rasa*—unsullied as yet by society. Poets of the period, including William Wordsworth, William Blake, and Samuel Taylor Coleridge, suggested that children in their guilelessness were closer to nature than adults. Obviously, their shared innocence and purity aligned children with the unicorn. Earlier myths insisted that children could see and touch the mythical creature because their vision had not been blinkered by doubt, and because the unicorn sensed that children were kindred spirits. The age-old "virgin" connection intimates that not only people who are sexually chaste, but those whose hearts and minds are pure can transcend the ordinary world and experience the mystical one. Who better than children to cross over into this wondrous territory?

The Valiant Little Tailor

"The Valiant Little Tailor" in the Grimms's early collection of fairy tales introduces children to the legend of tricking a unicorn into trapping itself (see Chapter 6). The story tells of a young tailor who squashes seven flies at one time, and then begins boasting of having killed "seven at one stroke." Proud of himself, the boy decides to journey into the larger world and finally arrives at the royal palace. Believing the tailor had slain seven *men* with one blow, the king engages him to kill two troublesome giants. The boy tricks the giants into killing each other, then returns to the palace to claim his reward: the hand of the princess.

The king, however, demands that before the boy can marry the princess he must capture the unicorn that lives in the forest. Taking a rope and an axe with him, the young tailor ventures into the woods where he soon comes upon the fabled creature. He stands in front of a large tree as the unicorn charges. At the last moment, the tailor jumps aside and the unicorn rushes headlong into the tree, driving his horn so deeply into the tree trunk that he can't pull it out. The boy slips the rope around the unicorn's neck, then chops away at the tree until he frees the beast's horn. Then he leads the unicorn back to the king. After completing one more trial, the king rewards the little tailor with the hand of the princess and half the kingdom, and there he reigns for the rest of his life.

Fanciful Eavesdroppers

In his fin-de-siècle collection of short stories, *The Lion and the Unicorn*, Richard Harding Davis introduces an amusing twist to the convention of placing figures of the lion and the unicorn—symbols of the United Kingdom—on London storefronts. What most people assume to be merely decorative depictions of animals, Davis tells us, are anything but. In fact, they oversee everything that goes on in the shops and streets from their elevated position. "By stretching a little, each of them could see into the window just beyond him, and could hear all that was said inside." Thus, the lion and the unicorn were privy to the gossip and goings-on of the time.

French Unicorn Fairy Tales

Late in the nineteenth century, F. Heuckenkamp edited an old French story based on the Arthurian legends, titled *Le Chevalier du Papegau*. In it, a young King Arthur meets a dwarf who lives in the forest with his infant son and a female unicorn. The unicorn hunts stags and other woodland animals for the dwarf to eat, killing them with her razor-sharp horn, and helps him build a hut from the boughs of trees. She even nurses the child with milk so rich and nourishing that the boy grows up to be a giant. Over time, the bond that develops between the unicorn and the boy becomes so strong that she follows him everywhere he goes like a pet. The story switches gender roles, giving a twist to the familiar legend of a young girl taming a male unicorn.

Another tale tells of sitting down at the dinner table to enjoy a meal with a unicorn. Before eating, however, the unicorn checked its own horn to see if it perspired—for as everyone knew in those days, if sweat beaded up on a unicorn's horn it meant the food was poisoned. In yet another story, the virgin-huntress Diana of Roman mythology (see Chapter 9) transforms a character into a unicorn as punishment for falling in love with a nymph. While he gazes at his beautiful reflection in the river, his nymph lover shoots him with an arrow and turns him into the River Sieve.

ROMANTIC AND VICTORIAN ARTISTS PAINT THE UNICORN

The Romantic and Victorian Eras oozed sensuality—at least in terms of art. Lush, evocative, vibrant, exquisitely beautiful paintings flowed from the brushes of painters such as John William Waterhouse, John Singer Sargent, Frederic Leighton, and Gustave Moreau. These artists took classical and mythological themes and interpreted them for eighteenth-century and nineteenth-century viewers. At the time, it was considered scandalous to depict ordinary women nude, but perfectly okay to show deities and other supernatural beings unclothed—which is what these artists did.

Moreau's *Jupiter and Europa*, for example, portrays the nude goddess with a strange creature whose body resembles a horse—except it has cloven hooves and a human head that looks very much like our conceptions of Jesus. Rays of light stream from the beast's head, suggesting a halo or crown and graphically linking the unicorn with Christ, as per early legends.

In his later work *The Unicorns*, Moreau painted a group of women and girls dressed in aristocratic finery on an outing with their pet unicorns. A nude woman lies amongst the group—perhaps some sort of deity, although she wears an elegant red velvet hat and appears to have recently shed the red gown on which she reclines. The females in the picture stroke the unicorns affectionately, which we might assume indicates their virginity. However, the nude, the royally clad lady in the foreground, and another in the background are decked out in red—a color traditionally used to signify passion and sensuality.

According to Ted Gott, Senior Curator of International Art for the National Gallery of Victoria in Melbourne (where Moreau's paintings were exhibited in 2011), "Throughout his life Moreau was both entranced by female beauty and captivated by the allure of powerful, even dangerous women from the pages of history and legend, making him a cult figure for today's younger generation who are spellbound by gothic tales and imagery." Dr. Gerard Vaughan, Director of the National Gallery of Australia, says, "Moreau's pictures are amongst the most haunting and mysterious of the entire 19th century, and ironically are incredibly modern."

John Waterhouse's painting *The Lady Clare* depicts Clare of the Temerin family and the sister of Arnaut de Cervole, a

French mercenary soldier during the Hundred Years' War. In 1357, the lady was hanged in the village of Castlegard and became a martyr. Alfred, Lord Tennyson penned her story poetically in 1842, and in it he describes a unicorn. Half a century later, Waterhouse recalled the virgin-unicorn connection by portraying Clare with a dainty white "doe" at her side that, alas, lacks a horn. Interestingly, the artist also chose to dress Lady Clare in a red gown.

> "He does not love me for my birth
>
> Nor for my lands so broad and fair;
>
> He loves me for my own true worth,
>
> And that is well," said Lady Clare.
>
> For, were I to learn his love was scorn,
>
> That he counts my wealth the greater part
>
> I'd take my pet's most toxic horn
>
> And drive it through his faithless heart."

—Alfred, Lord Tennyson

Lady Clare's tale is told again in Michael Crichton's thriller *Timeline* and Richard Donner's 2003 sci-fi film, based on the book. In the modern-day version's storyline, archaeologists from 1999 end up time-traveling back to France in 1357, where they find themselves embroiled in the travails of the period.

VICTORIAN FEMMES FATALES

e often look back at the Victorian era, named for England's Queen Victoria who reigned from 1837 until 1901, as a time of sexual repression and uptight, moralistic stuffiness. The accepted mores for women at the time support that view, as do the period's "cover everything" fashions that rival Muslim burqas (except for the corset-cinched waists favored by the Victorians). In those days, as in earlier times, women were considered temptresses who had to be restrained—just a glimpse of ladies' bare ankles or unbound hair might cause men to lose control of themselves.

Ensnaring the Unicorn

The Victorians' opinion of women was reflected in their interpretation of the myth of the unicorn and the virgin. During this era, people began to scrutinize the lady in the legend, more so than the unicorn itself—and not in a nice way. The maiden girl was no longer considered innocent, helpless "bait" for the unicorn, but a dangerous partner in crime who was complicit in the beast's capture. Now she was portrayed as a conniving vixen and the unicorn as her naïve prey. According to the nineteenth-century Massachusetts scholar Thomas Bulfinch, once the unicorn approached her and laid his head in her lap, "The treacherous virgin then gave a signal, and the hunters made in and captured the simple beast."

A Feminist Perspective on the Unicorn Myth

The first wave of feminism—or the Woman Question, as it was called then—arose in the late nineteenth century, as women on both sides of the Atlantic began to show displeasure with the limited role society had allocated to them and the constraints placed upon them by male-dominated culture. Women sought greater freedom and equality in political and financial areas, as well as in sexual ones. A woman's right to make decisions regarding her own body—an issue that continues to spark debate today—had its parallels in the unicorn-virgin myth. Women started asking questions:

- Why was the unicorn interested only in virgins?
- Why was chastity valued in women, whereas for men the issue was a moot point?
- If the innocent male unicorn falls for the female virgin because he recognizes her as a kindred spirit as pure as himself, shouldn't the myth advise men as well as women to remain physically pure in the real world as well as in fantasyland?

Once again, a mythic creature whose cloven feet may never have touched down on Planet Earth became a mirror for its human counterparts. As a sign of the times and a symbol of socio-political-religious ideology, the unicorn reveals more about us than it does about itself.

The Unicorn Goes to War

Although we usually think of the unicorn as a peaceful creature, Britain's Royal Navy named a thirty-two-gun fighting frigate the HMS *Unicorn* and launched her in 1794. She served in the French Revolutionary War and the Napoleonic Wars. Her military career ended in 1815.

THE UNICORN ACCORDING TO DUVAUCEL

In 1817, the French naturalist Alfred Duvaucel traveled to Calcutta to collect plant and animal specimens for the Paris Museum of Natural History. He'd been there a few years when he heard news that unicorns had been discovered at the Cape of Good Hope and in the mountains of Bhutan. Duvaucel wrote a letter to the editor of the *Calcutta Journal,* (September 20, 1821) and signed it A.D. Credule, Voyageur aux Grandes Indes. Ten months later, *Blackwood's Edinburgh Magazine* published the letter (quoted here in part):

"While traversing the mountains of Gentya, to the north of Sylhet, [Bangladesh] I at first discovered a very extraordinary tooth . . . and afterwards a horn, two feet, three inches, and five lines in length, which does not belong to any known antelope. On the following day I perceived the impression of a cloven hoof, like that of a stag; and the Rajah of Gentyapour, who is a keen naturalist, has made me a present of a small bit of skin covered with coarse hair, which assuredly is the hair of a unicorn," wrote Duvaucel, believing that he had found evidence of the unicorn. He then questioned the locals and recounted their descriptions of unicorns, which they called the *Boracrack*.

"The natives of Cossya [India] assert, that during the first year the unicorn is white, spotted with black; that, during the second year, the spots disappear, and the hair becomes grey; the third year it varies from sky-blue to metallic-green; the fourth it assumes a yellowish tint; and the fifth, the period at which the animal attains its full growth, its fur is of a bright red, which becomes lighter in proportion as age advances, and this in such a manner, that on seeing the unicorn one may determine its age with considerable accuracy . . .

"These animals are furnished with so prodigious a degree of strength in their hind legs, that they can, without difficulty, clear a ditch of eighty feet; but what is no less worthy of attention is their wonderful address in the use of their horn, with which they spit squirrels, rabbits, and partridges, which, together with grass, and the leaves and bark of certain trees, form their habitual food!!!"

He included a sketch of the beast, which was not reproduced in the magazine. "Besides, why not believe in the unicorn, when every thing concurs to prove its existence? We have a one-horned rhinoceros in India, and why should there not also be a one-horned antelope?"

Duvaucel insisted, "It would be an easy matter for me, Sir, to collect as many proofs of the existence of unicorns, and cite more than twenty celebrated travellers who have seen them . . .

"I hope that the natives of Cossya, or those of Africa, or those of Thibet, or the researches that are making in Nepaul, and on the coast of Sumatra, will soon procure for us a dozen of unicorns, and the pleasure of laughing at the expense of naturalists."

CHAPTER 9

New Twists to Old Tales: Modern Unicorn Myths

"Nothing is more magical . . . As long as they roam the Earth, evil cannot harm the pure of heart."

—From the movie *Legend*

IN EARLIER TIMES, myths and legends about unicorns were intended for adult audiences. Not until the last century or so have storytellers aimed tales of these magical creatures at children and young people.

Today's unicorns are both lighter and darker than their predecessors. Perhaps that's because our world seems scary, violent, and chaotic, and often we feel powerless to change or control things. Consequently, contemporary writers and artists choose either to weave the darkness they perceive in modern society into their unicorn sagas or, conversely, to present the unicorn in a more light-hearted and whimsical way. For as everyone knows, the unicorn is a symbol of hope.

Some things never change, however. The timeless themes of growing from innocence to wisdom, courage and loyalty in the face of danger, and the triumph of good over evil, honor over treachery, delight us just as much today as they did our ancestors a thousand years ago.

MIXING MYTHS

The 1985 film *Legend*, directed by Ridley Scott and starring Tom Cruise, combines the basic themes of traditional unicorn mythology with those of vampire tales. In it, the villain is a thoroughly evil fellow aptly named Lord of Darkness who lives in an underground castle and comes out only at night because he can't bear being exposed to sunlight. The Lord of Darkness plans to destroy the last two unicorns still surviving on earth, because once the pure and gentle creatures disappear so will the light in the world—allowing the demonic Lord to move about wherever he pleases unscathed. He sends three goblins named Blix, Pox, and Blunder to kill the unicorns and bring their magic horns to him.

The good guys in the film are Jack (played by Tom Cruise) and his girlfriend Lili (Mia Sara), along with a group of fairies they meet in the forest. Jack takes Lili to see a mated pair of unicorns, and she makes the mistake of patting the male (signifying her chastity).

While the unicorn is in her thrall, the nasty Blix shoots it with a poisoned arrow. As soon as the goblins cut off the dying unicorn's horn, winter descends upon the earth.

Lili, feeling horribly guilty due to her part in the male unicorn's death, tries to find and protect his mate. But the goblins capture her and the female unicorn and take them to Lord of Darkness's castle. While Jack and his fairy friends make their way to the castle, the dastardly Lord of Darkness attempts to seduce Lili and thereby nullify her power to help the remaining unicorn.

Jack and his buddies end up imprisoned in the basement of the evil Lord's castle where they discover they're scheduled for dinner—not as guests, but as the main course. Lord of Darkness, it seems, doesn't merely drink the blood of his victims like a regular vampire, he actually eats them. However, as in all good fairy tales, the heroes escape and manage to revive the dead unicorn by reattaching his horn.

Legend also mixes in another familiar fairy tale element, this time from *Sleeping Beauty.* It seems the Lord of Darkness has cast a spell on Lili, rendering her unconscious. Only her beloved's kiss, and the return of a ring she tossed into a pond before all the mayhem started, can awaken her. All ends happily, except for one little problem—Darkness isn't dead and he wants revenge.

Ridley Scott seems to have a thing about unicorns. In Scott's earlier sci-fi film *Blade Runner*, a police officer named Gaff uses an origami unicorn made of aluminum foil as his significator. You can purchase a handmade reproduction of the metallic creature from Kenneth Thompson at *www.bladerunnerunicorn.com.*

Mixed-Up Mythology

The Urban Dictionary mentions a bizarre beast called a "vampire unicorn," a mix of the two mythic species. According to the Dictionary's humorous definition, these creatures ". . . only come out at night to suck the blood of unsuspecting victims, while jumping over rainbows. They live in candy mountain, and are on the endangered species list because meth-zombie poachers are always shooting them . . . a horn from a vampire unicorn can go for as much as 6 grams of meth."

THE LADY *IS* THE UNICORN

The 1982 fantasy film *The Last Unicorn* also focuses on the end of the unicorn as a species on earth—and it also mixes in another legend, that of Hans Christian Andersen's story "The Little Mermaid." Based on Peter S. Beagle's 1968 book, the heroine of this beautifully animated movie reminds us of the graceful white unicorn in the Renaissance tapestries (see Chapter 6). The film features the voices of Alan Arkin, Jeff Bridges, and Mia Farrow as the unicorn.

Although most classic legends speak primarily of male unicorns, this one stars a female whose fellows have all been driven into the ocean by a beastly creature known as the Red Bull. The lonely unicorn embarks on a quest to find her friends and relatives, but along the way she gets captured and placed in a carnival.

With the help of a wizard named Schmendrick, the unicorn manages to escape and journeys on toward the castle of King Haggard (voiced by Christopher Lee), home of the ferocious Red

Bull—and runs right into the monster. To save her, Schmendrick transforms the unicorn into a woman with long white hair, who holds no appeal for the Red Bull. When they reach the castle where the king lives with his son Prince Lir, Schmendrick introduces the former unicorn as his niece, Lady Amalthea. Amalthea falls in love with the prince and, like the Little Mermaid, she considers sacrificing her true magical nature for human love.

Eventually, the Red Bull discovers that Amalthea isn't what she seems, so Schmendrick turns her back into a unicorn and the Red Bull chases her toward the sea. When Prince Lir tries to protect her, the bull kills him. Of course, as we know, unicorns can cure all manner of illness and even raise the dead (à la stories about Jesus), which is exactly what she does in this case. Again, we see a parallel to the Little Mermaid, who rescues the drowning prince with whom she falls in love. As the unicorn attacks the Red Bull and drives him into the ocean, all the other unicorns gain their freedom and gallop off toward the forest. The "last unicorn" goes with them, carrying with her the mixed blessing of having experienced life and love as a human.

More Unicorns from Beagle

Peter S. Beagle followed up *The Last Unicorn* with *The Unicorn Sonata*. Though not a sequel to the first book, it contains much of the same magic that made *The Last Unicorn* so compelling a story. A contemporary Los Angeles girl, Joey Rivera, enters the magical world of Shei'rah, where the unicorns are suffering from blindness. Beagle also produced an anthology of short stories, *Immortal Unicorn*.

"The unicorn lived in a lilac wood, and she lived all alone. She was very old, though she did not know it, and she was no longer the careless colour of sea foam, but rather the colour of snow falling on a moonlit night."

—Peter S. Beagle, *The Last Unicorn*

THE UNICORN AND THE VIRGIN

The age-old myth of the unicorn and the virgin continues to provide contemporary authors with inspiration for novels, stories, plays, and movies. Usually, however, modern writers examine the myth from a psychological or sociological perspective, rather than a religious one.

The Glass Unicorn

In Tennessee Williams's 1944 play *The Glass Menagerie*, the character Laura is represented by her favorite item in her prized collection: a glass unicorn. Laura—like the supposedly extinct unicorn—is gentle, naive, and pure. When the character Jim dances with the sheltered Laura and kisses her, the glass unicorn's horn breaks off. This suggests that her metaphorical chastity is destroyed, and that as a result, she becomes an ordinary creature—no longer a rarified being, just another horse. But it also indicates that Laura cannot become "normal" and move into the adult world of male-female relationships unless she transcends her childlike innocence.

À Mon Seul Désir

In her novel *Guinevere*, Sharan Newman writes about a devoted unicorn who, like all unicorns, has a thing for virgins. But this particular beast is faithful to one virgin only: the Lady Guinevere, who is destined to become the wife of King Arthur. Newman tells the story of the youthful Guinevere, a beautiful and charming girl, and the unicorn who loves her exclusively. Newman's psychological portrait also recounts the theme of "courtly love" (see Chapter 1), which decreed that a knight or nobleman pledge himself solely to a lady of the court—a relationship symbolized in legend by the unicorn and the virgin. When Guinevere marries Arthur and loses her virginity, the unicorn in Newman's story dies. The virgin-unicorn theme, as Newman interprets it, is doubly intriguing because in the Arthurian Legends, Guinevere is usually cast as an unfaithful wife who cheats on her husband with his best friend, Sir Lancelot.

The Cluny Tapestries Revisited

Best-selling author Tracy Chevalier weaves her 2004 novel *The Lady and the Unicorn* around the famous Renaissance tapestries known as *Lady and the Unicorn* (or the Cluny tapestries, see Chapter 6). The tapestries portray the well-known virgin-unicorn myth, organized around the theme of the five senses. In Chevalier's story, an artist named Nicolas des Innocents (who's anything but what his name suggests) is hired by a French nobleman, Jean Le Viste, to design a series of intricate tapestries. Jean's wife, Geneviève, convinces the artist to create six panels that feature a lady taming a unicorn—with herself and her daughter Claude as his models. Nicolas, symbolizing the unicorn, falls in love with Claude, who represents the virgin in the myth. This modern adaptation of an old legend examines the conflict between love and duty, as well as social power and the class structure of the Gothic era in Europe.

Reinterpreting an Arthurian Legend

T.H. White, in his novel *The Once and Future King*, revisits the legend of King Arthur and the long-standing connection between knights and the unicorn—but not in the usual manner. In White's tale, three brothers named for the legendary knights Gareth, Gawaine, and Agravaine, go out into the forest in search of a unicorn. Their mother, a Gaelic woman named Morgause (who's usually depicted in the legends as Morgana or Morgan le Fey, Arthur's half-sister and a sorceress), organizes hunting parties and the three young men hope to please her by killing a unicorn. They manage to find and slay the rare creature and take its head back

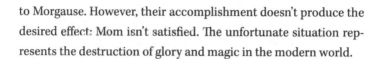
to Morgause. However, their accomplishment doesn't produce the desired effect: Mom isn't satisfied. The unfortunate situation represents the destruction of glory and magic in the modern world.

Engineering a Unicorn

Gene Wolfe's 1980 story "The Woman the Unicorn Loved" brings together many of the familiar unicorn myths and merges them into a sci-fi tale. The story's protagonist, literature professor Dr. Anderson, spots a white horse with red hooves trotting across campus, and hurries down to get a closer look. A crowd has gathered around the creature, but Anderson and his colleague Dr. Dumont push through to see the beast. Dumont tries to feed it white bread, as per an old English nursery rhyme, but Anderson knows his mythology and realizes that only a virgin female can touch a unicorn. A young graduate student named Julie takes the bread and gives it to the unicorn, while stroking its horn. But soon the police arrive and scare the animal away.

The unicorn, it seems, has resulted from a college experiment to genetically modify a horse. Captivated with the magnificent creature, Julie locks it in the library in the fantasy section, with the aid of Bailey the night watchman—unbeknownst to Anderson and Dumont. But when Bailey goes to check on it, the unicorn gores him to death and runs away to another part of the building. After finding the watchman's body, Anderson and Dumont—armed with a tranquilizer gun—go in search of the dangerous animal. They hope that by opening the building's doors and offering the unicorn freedom, it will take the bait and they can tranquilize and capture it, instead of calling in the police.

However, when Anderson kisses Julie, the unicorn charges in a jealous rage and knocks the professor to the floor. It kicks and drags Anderson, breaking his leg, and then escapes to the lake, where legend tells us unicorns go at dawn to purify the waters.

Throughout the tale the characters quote from various literary sources, and Professor Anderson explains the history, myths, and speculations about the unicorn. The author discusses biblical references to the creature, Pliny's mistaken identification of a rhinoceros as a unicorn, the hoax of the narwhal's horn, even the English nursery rhyme about the fight between the lion and the unicorn that we've talked about in previous chapters of this book. If you're looking for a crash course in unicorn mythology, "The Woman the Unicorn Loved" is a good place to start.

Hunting Unicorns in Michigan

In 1971, Bill Rabe, then Director of Public Relations for Lake Superior State University in Sault Ste. Marie, Michigan, established the Unicorn Hunters to garner publicity for the school. The Unicorn Hunters issued hunting licenses to unicorn seekers, and established a set of regulations that allowed questers to bag only one male unicorn per month using the approved weapons of serious intent, iambic pentameter, general levity, or sweet talk. Of course, the only acceptable bait was a virgin.

Virgin Unicorn Hunters

Diana Peterfreund, author of the Killer Unicorns series (*Rampant, Ascendant,* and *Errant*), gives a new twist to an old tale. Her unicorns aren't the docile, shy, peace-loving creatures history describes—they're dangerous, and must be hunted down and destroyed. But these deadly beasts can be killed only by the virgin descendants of Alexander the Great—remember, he's supposedly the only person who ever actually rode a unicorn.

As discussed in Chapter 6, Peterfreund also questions the conventional interpretation of the word "virginity." Historically, "virgin" has referred to a woman who has never engaged in sexual intercourse with a man. But what about lesbians, who may be sexually active, just not with male partners? Or women who retain their "maidenheads" while performing other sex acts? In a 2010 interview with fellow author Malinda Lo, Peterfreund explains, "the magic in my book [*Ascendant*] is a metaphor for this patriarchal system."

Diana and Artemis

Among the many deities in ancient mythology we find the moon goddess and virgin huntress Diana (Roman) a.k.a. Artemis (Greek). She's usually depicted as a protector of animals, an independent and rather wild character who carries a bow and quiver full of arrows. Sometimes artists picture her with a deer or her hunting dogs as companions. Stories tell of her hunting the stag, a symbol of masculinity. Additionally, she's the patron goddess of women and girl children. According to myth, she never had a male lover and rejected marriage, preferring to remain free. Her earthly priests and priestess took vows of chastity, and were punished— sometimes by death—if they transgressed.

In 1971, California author, witch, and feminist activist Z Budapest founded the first coven of The Dianic Feminist Wicca/Witchcraft Tradition. Dianic Wicca is a woman/goddess-centered spiritual path and emphasizes feminist ideals. Many Dianic covens admit only women and some attract only lesbians, but that's not true in all cases.

UNICORNS IN AN AGE OF FEAR AND VIOLENCE

ld myths and legends almost always portray the unicorn as a gentle, shy, and kindhearted creature. Even today, these beloved creatures retain their traditional nature in many stories. Historically, unicorns have possessed deadly power and wielded their horns as weapons when necessary, but only to protect themselves or those they love. The fact that such a fearsome lance could belong to such a peaceful creature is part of the unicorn's enticing irony.

Some contemporary authors, however, show unicorns in a different light: as malevolent creatures that pose a danger to humans and/or other animals. At a time when fear and violence seem omnipresent in our world, we find unicorns playing both roles—sometimes as peacekeepers heroically striving to defeat evil, and sometimes as demonic beings you certainly wouldn't want your kids to hang out with.

UNICORN SIGHTINGS

Ted Andrews, author of *Treasures of the Unicorn* and numerous other books, recalls a day in his youth when he encountered a unicorn at a pond near his childhood home. "The weeds rustled softly and the faint tinkling of bells sounded again. It stepped out to the pond's edge. I gasped. My eyes widened. It was not a deer that had stepped from the tall weeds. It was a magnificent unicorn! It turned its head toward me at the sound of my gasp and held me fixed with its sparkling, blue eyes. I didn't move. I didn't blink. I didn't even breathe. I just stared, wide-eyed . . .

"The horn stood strong in the center of the unicorn's head and had what seemed a spiral marking, shimmering with a silver tint in the early morning light. The unicorn's coat seemed to shift in color and brilliance, depending upon how it caught the light, sometimes white, sometimes silver. A soft haze surrounded the animal.

"Keeping its eyes fixed upon me, the unicorn bent its front legs, and lowered the horn to the surface of the pond. As the point touched the pond's surface, I heard the soft tinkling of the bells again . . . The surface of the water bubbled like it was being brought to a boil and ripples spread outward from the unicorn's horn tip . . .

"I left my perch and moved slowly around the edge of the pond to where I had seen the unicorn. All that remained of its presence was half of a hoof print and several weeds bent but unbroken."

Peace-Loving Unicorns

Award-winning author Roger Zelazny uses two familiar symbols—the unicorn and the snake—in his fiction series The Chronicles of Amber. The tales present two opposing worlds: Amber, and The Courts of Chaos. Naturally, the unicorn represents peace and order (Amber), whereas the snake—the ancient symbol of evil and the unicorn's nemesis—signifies Chaos.

Beer, Chess, and Unicorns

In 1983, Zelazny was asked to contribute to three different fiction anthologies: one featuring unicorns, one of stories set in taverns, and one about chess. Zelazny opted to combine the three themes and penned a tale about a chess-playing unicorn that enjoyed a cold brewski. His story "Unicorn Variations" won the Hugo Award, given for works of science fiction, and became part of a book by the same title.

Madeleine L'Engle's protagonist Charles Wallace, in her 1978 novel *A Swiftly Tilting Planet*, summons a unicorn for help on the eve of nuclear war. The unicorn tells Wallace he must travel back in time and change the course of events in the past, in order to avert the upcoming war. Wallace rides a unicorn named Gaudior, who symbolizes peace and joy, back through the ages—Wallace even gets to visit the unicorn hatching grounds and see baby unicorns. What a lucky guy!

The unicorns in Piers Anthony's fantasy series Apprentice Adept are portrayed as magical shapeshifters, who can assume the forms of other creatures. In addition, these talented beings play their horns as musical instruments. Unlike the usual depiction of unicorns as pure-white animals, Anthony's unicorns come in various colors and combinations. Clip, for instance, is blue with red socks—and he can take off the socks if he chooses.

Author Bruce Coville, in his series The Unicorn Chronicles, escorts us into the Land of Luster, the world where the unicorns live. *Into the Land of Unicorns,* the first book in the series, tells the story of a girl named Cara Diana Hunter who travels to Luster and befriends the unicorn Lightfoot—combining the myth of the Roman virgin hunter-goddess Diana with the ancient legend of the maiden and the unicorn. Lightfoot accompanies her in her quest to save Luster and the unicorns from destruction. Later novels follow Cara through Luster as she faces danger in various forms, including one of her own ancestors whose goal is to wipe unicorns off the face of the earth. That ancestor, named Beloved, is immortal like the unicorns because she bears a bit of a unicorn's horn in her heart.

Plenty of other peace-loving unicorns gallop across the pages of contemporary fantasy novels and movie screens, carrying on the tradition of their gentle predecessors. But today's tales also introduce us to a different brand of unicorns who may scare, harm, or even eat you if they get the chance.

A Glory of Unicorns

You've heard of a gaggle of geese, a pride of lions, and a murder of crows, right? Well, what's a group of unicorns called? A "glory." Author Bruce Coville coined the term and wrote a novel about them, titled *A Glory of Unicorns.*

Dangerous Unicorn Liaisons

As discussed earlier, you don't want to snuggle up with the unicorns in Diana Peterfreund's Killer Unicorns series if you hope to see the next sunrise. These ferocious beasts come armed with poisonous horns and fangs—and they like to feast on human flesh. But as the author explains, the unicorns aren't inherently evil. "These unicorns are animals and they are following a survival instinct. They are living in a world that is incredibly unsuited for them—world of cities and highways and people who don't want to be eaten. However, that doesn't mean they don't kill for reasons other than food—any animals kill over territory or protective instincts." Peterfreund's protagonist, a sixteen-year-old virgin huntress named Astrid (which means "divine strength" in Norse), must determine which unicorns are dangerous and must be removed for the good of all. She also must consider other ways of protecting the people she loves without killing the unicorns.

The 2010 short-story anthology *Zombies vs. Unicorns* pits the two pop-culture creatures against each other in a literary "war." Edited by Holly Black and Justine Larbalestier, the collection includes tales penned by a number of fantasy and horror authors. Although some stories in the anthology present unicorns in their traditional role as good guys, others, including Margo Lanagan's "A Thousand Flowers," take a dark turn. Lanagan switches the unicorn's usual role—instead of being a devotee of the virgin he's a rapist. The princess he takes advantage of births a human-unicorn hybrid baby, and when the strange creature dies, the princess commits suicide. "The Third Virgin" by Kathleen Duey is told from the perspective of the unicorn, and addresses the unicorn's legendary power to heal the sick. In this dark tale, however, the unicorn has grown addicted to its power to make life-and-death decisions.

In Tanith Lee's novel *Black Unicorn*, a mechanically adept girl and her witchy mother manage to resurrect a long-dead unicorn from its skeleton. If that weren't creepy enough, the beast then starts stalking the daughter.

A Killer Idea

Director Drew Goddard must have had fun making the 2012 horror comedy *The Cabin in the Woods*, which features a killer unicorn (obviously a white horse with a horn stuck on its head) that plays against type. During the animal's escape from a secret facility that houses monsters, the unicorn gores a character in the stomach. Despite the fact that the story sounds pretty hokey, the movie got positive reviews from most sectors. Oh, and by the way, don't mess with that unicorn tapestry stuffed away in the basement . . .

These and other contemporary tales veer away from the conventional conceptions we hold about unicorns and our relationship with them. Some stories raise hypothetical "what if" questions, whereas others look at unicorns in the context of the world in which they must live now—a world that has changed drastically since the unicorn's glory days back in the Renaissance— and how our modern world affects them.

THE LION AND THE UNICORN

All the way back to ancient Babylon, mythology and folklore portray the lion and the unicorn as enemies (see Chapter 6). Both Eastern and Western tales describe the animosity between the two beasts. Stories even tell us that Noah couldn't rescue both creatures because they'd fight on the Ark. On the United Kingdom's coat of arms, the lion and the unicorn represent England and Scotland respectively, symbolizing their union in 1603, but only after a long and bitter period of conflict.

"Jewel was so gentle and soft of speech that, if you hadn't known, you would hardly have believed how fierce and terrible he could be in battle."

—C.S. Lewis

The Land of Narnia

In The Chronicles of Narnia, a series of seven novels about a fanciful kingdom inhabited by all sorts of peculiar creatures, author C.S. Lewis chose to turn the tables on the old idea of the lion and the unicorn as rivals. Instead, Lewis's character Jewel, a creamy-white unicorn with an icy-blue horn, is a loyal and devoted friend to Alsan, a godly lion and the One True King of the land of Narnia.

In Lewis's *The Last Battle*, an ambitious ape named Shift wants to ascend to power in Narnia. He convinces a donkey named Puzzle to dress up in a lion's pelt and impersonate the lion Aslan. As the plot thickens, Jewel is captured and ordered to proclaim that the False Aslan (the donkey Puzzle) is real—but the honorable unicorn refuses, even when threatened with death. Attempting to save Narnia, Jewel charges into battle, using his magical horn as a weapon.

The Real-Life Children of Narnia

C.S. Lewis, an Englishman, wrote his Narnia tales not long after the end of World War II. Three children, who had been evacuated from London during the war and relocated near Lewis's home just outside Oxford, served as inspiration for the main characters in his series of fantasy stories.

Looking-Glass Land

In Lewis Carroll's amusing and delightful *Through the Looking-Glass and What Alice Found There*, Alice meets a king and his Anglo-Saxon messenger Haigha while wandering in the forest. The messenger reports that the lion and the unicorn are fighting again. As an old English nursery rhyme tells us, the two creatures are fighting over the crown—a battle that represents the war between England and Scotland (see Chapter 6). It seems the contest is a waste of time, however, for as the king in Carroll's tale explains, no matter who wins neither will get his crown.

The three characters go off to watch the animals fight, arriving just as the lion and the unicorn decide to take a break for refreshments: white bread and brown, as per the nursery rhyme. The unicorn trots over to the King, and suddenly spots Alice.

" 'What—is—this?' he said at last.

'This is a child!' Haigha replied eagerly, coming in front of Alice to introduce her, and spreading out both his hands toward her in an Anglo-Saxon attitude. 'We only found it to-day. It's as large as life, and twice as natural!'

'I always thought they were fabulous monsters!' said the Unicorn. 'Is it alive?'

'It can talk,' said Haigha solemnly.

The Unicorn looked dreamily at Alice, and said 'Talk, child.'

Alice could not help her lips curling up into a smile as she began: 'Do you know, I always thought Unicorns were fabulous monsters, too? I never saw one alive before!'

'Well, now that we *have* seen each other,' said the Unicorn, 'if you'll believe in me, I'll believe in you. Is that a bargain?'"

WILL UNICORNS EXIST IN THE FUTURE?

If Hanville Svetz has anything to do with it, unicorns will continue to fascinate us for a long, long time. In Larry Niven's humorous sci-fi story "The Flight of the Horse" the halfwit son of the Secretary-General sees a picture of a horse in an ancient children's book and wants one for his twenty-eighth birthday. So a young man named Hanville Svetz is ordered to travel back in time to the planet earth to capture the animal, which has been extinct for 1,000 years. Upon arriving, Svetz sees a creature that looks pretty much like the horse in the picture book, except instead of being brown this one is pure white—and it has a long projectile jutting out from the middle of its forehead.

The strange beast is also a whole lot larger, stronger, and faster than anything Svetz had imagined. He chases it in his flying machine, but the horse outdistances him easily. Despite the animal's wildness, however, it behaves like a tame pet when it comes near a tiny young girl. Svetz figures it must be her horse, so instead of killing it he trades her numerous valuable gemstones for the creature. With her help, he manages to get the unicorn into his time machine. A struggle ensues, during which the frightened animal nearly skewers Svetz "like a cocktail shrimp" with its horn.

Somehow, the time machine succeeds in returning both Svetz and the unicorn back to the future, where the physicians and scientists are amazed at the creature's strength and stamina. Svetz had seen it drink from a poisonous pond on earth and the doctors discover " 'over fifty unknown varieties of bacteria in the beast's bloodstream. Yet it hardly looked sick! It looked healthy as a . . . healthy as a . . .' "

But the horn presents a problem. Not only is it a dangerous and potentially lethal weapon, the horse in the ancient picture book didn't have a horn. Therefore, the Director of the Institute for Temporal Research decides to amputate the horn before giving the unicorn to the Secretary-General. Svetz can't bear to see the beautiful creature mutilated, so he proposes that they alter the children's book instead—then all the horses in it will have horns. Which is exactly what they do.

The ruse is so successful that the Director sends young Svetz back to earth again, this time in search of a Gila monster. "The thing he brought back was thirty feet long, had vestigial batlike wings, breathed fire, and didn't look very much like the illustration; but it was as close as anything he'd found. The Secretary-General loved it."

The Three Stooges Meet a Unicorn

Space travel was all the rage in 1959, when Columbia Pictures released *Have Rocket, Will Travel* starring The Three Stooges: Curly, Larry, and Moe. In the zany comedy film, the trio accidentally launch themselves into space where they befriend a talking unicorn.

Larry: "Ain't he quaint?"
Moe: " 'Ain't'? The word is 'isn't'!"
Larry: "Isn't he quisn't?"

Our relationship with the unicorn could change in the future, if writer Terry Pratchett is right. His 1992 novel *Lords and Ladies,* the fourteenth in his Discworld series, is a tale of parallel universes, witches, and elves (bad guys whose powers diminish when they're exposed to iron). In it, the crone character Granny Weatherwax plays farrier and shoes a unicorn. Although the act suggests that she tames the unicorn, she doesn't wish to weaken or dominate him by hammering ordinary iron horseshoes onto his hooves.

Instead, she gives him silver shoes, silver being the moon's metal, and mythology links the unicorn with the moon.

As Helen Pilinovsky, PhD, former professor at Pacific University Oregon, explains, this symbolic act allows the unicorn "to coexist in harmony with mankind in a way in which it hadn't been allowed to in past iterations. The unicorn is no longer bound by the literal past mythology, where it has to die in order for humanity to benefit ... Today, our symbolism points to a hard-won détente: a truce between the magic of the unknown and the control of civilization."

CHAPTER 10

Unicorns in Popular Culture

"Instead of a motorcycle, why not ride a custom-engineered unicorn?
The unicorn could be genetically grown like corn."

—Jarod Kintz, *Seriously Delirious, But Not at All Serious*

IN SOME WAYS, kids today live more sheltered lives than their parents and grandparents did. Fifty years ago, boys and girls didn't wear bicycle helmets or seatbelts or go on play dates scheduled for them by their moms. As modern-day parents attempt to protect their children from real or imagined dangers, the unicorn has been stripped of its wild, independent, and sometimes fierce nature. Its form has become cutsified, so that it looks like a darling little horse with big eyes and a colorful horn that couldn't pierce butter.

Its animalistic nature has disappeared, along with its lion's tail and goatish beard. Although the unicorns of yesteryear were usually male, females seem to have cornered today's toy market (even though folklore tells us female unicorns don't have horns). In short, the unicorn has been tamed—not by legendary virgins, but by the likes of Hasbro and Disney.

WHAT COLOR IS YOUR UNICORN?

We have Walt Disney to thank for our present-day ideas of unicorns: cute, cuddly creatures in pretty pastel colors, suitable for decorating little girls' backpacks and pajamas. In the 1940 landmark animated film *Fantasia*, Disney's adorable unicorns frolic across the screen, having a good time with their mythic buddies the centaurs and the satyrs. In some aspects, these fanciful animals resemble our earlier conceptions—they're horse-like, and of course display a single spiral-shaped horn. However, whereas unicorns in the previous few centuries were usually depicted as snow white to symbolize their purity, *Fantasia's* unicorns sported bright yellow horns and coats of pink, blue, and lavender.

Disney's film also strips the magical beast of the awesome power and majesty once attached to it. Now the unicorns appear friendly and playful, almost like toys—and indeed, the movie spawned a host of fluffy spinoffs. As director Mel Brooks points out in his comedy film *Spaceballs*, it's all about merchandising.

The Year of the Unicorn

In March 2015, the *Wall Street Journal* reported that toy manufacturers had declared 2015 the "year of the unicorn."

My Little Pony

In 1983, the Rhode Island-based toy and game company Hasbro, Inc. (originally Hassenfeld Brothers, after the two brothers who founded it) introduced a collection of adorable little plastic horses as toys for young girls. The line, dubbed "My Little Pony," included unicorns among its earliest offerings. Over the decades, the line evolved into plush toys, games, play stations, TV shows, movies, DVDs, apps, and more. Thirty-plus years after their inception, the ponies are still riding high. According to Reuters, Hasbro's sales of toys for girls rose by 21 percent in the first quarter of 2014 (compared with a 2 percent increase for toys aimed at boys), and strong demand for My Little Pony products helped boost revenues from toys for girls to nearly $140 million during that period.

The popular TV program *My Little Pony: Friendship Is Magic* starred a unicorn named Princess Twilight Sparkle, who looks more like a type of candy than a traditional unicorn. Purple with a rainbow-colored mane and tail, she also sprouts tiny wings. Hasbro's marketing team presents a whole new take on the unicorn's personality when it tells us, "Princess Twilight Sparkle is super smart and a natural born leader. She is good at helping her pony friends use their skills and talents to get the job done, while discovering new things about herself and all her amazing friends!" Really?

Hasbro's 2015 line of interactive, animatronic toys features a playful creature dubbed "Starlily, My Magical Unicorn" with wings that flutter and a horn that lights up in a rainbow of colors, in response to a little girl's touch. Feed Starlily, and she utters happy munching sounds. Sensors positioned at the unicorn's face enable her to perform almost like a real animal. With a price tag of $120, this cat-sized toy unicorn better do *something* to earn its keep.

"I think that if you have a horse, pegasus qilin, or unicorn, you should sit on it! You should stroke its hair, whisper in its ear, be one with it! And you shouldn't feel sorry if other people don't have one."

—C. JoyBell C., author

Barbie's Unicorns

Even though Barbie is pushing senior citizen status (Mattel introduced her back in 1959), she still keeps up with the times. Therefore, it's no surprise that fashion-conscious Barbie has her own pet unicorns as companions. Princess Unicorn (available in pink or purple) features a long, shimmering mane and tail, huge azure eyes, a sparkly horn, and a "gem"-encrusted saddle. Barbie's Secret Door Unicorn, designed to go along with her DVD, has flowers and butterflies tattooed on its flank. Little girls can gussy up the unicorn by adding colorful hair extensions and flowers to its mane and tail.

Princess Pretty Pants

Meg Cabot, author of the best-selling Princess Diaries series, contributed a story titled "Princess Pretty Pants" to the 2010 anthology *Zombies vs. Unicorns*. In it, Cabot's unicorns are so dainty, sweet, and pretty that when they fart, rainbows burst from their butts. Although Cabot may not be responsible for originating this particular trait among unicorns, apparently the idea holds great appeal for some, as a quick Google search will reveal. You can even buy a birthday cake decorated with the scene, guaranteed to make kids giggle. (Honestly, does that sound appetizing?)

Unicorns and Rainbows

The connection between unicorns and rainbows shows yet another example of mixed myths: that of the fanciful beast and that of the leprechaun's pot of gold at the end of the rainbow. According to the Urban Dictionary, the pairing means "a feeling of perpetual bliss; only to be described as pure happiness and satisfaction. It describes what it means to finally find your true happy ending." Alternately (and sarcastically), it refers to a "series of painful incidents or unfortunate experiences."

Unico

This darling baby unicorn from Japanese anime children's films looks more like a red-haired teddy bear with a spike on his head than the usual pony-type creature Western kids know and love. Like Disney and Hasbro's unicorns, however, he's a cheerful, sociable, and sweet little being who wants only to bring happiness to everyone he meets—he's totally devoid of the wild, fierce independence and solitary nature of legendary unicorns. The Unico movies mix in characters and lore from other cultures, including a Celtic-derived devil, a Sphinx, and a cat who wants to study magic and hang out with a witch, along with some from classical mythology including Psyche (Unico is her pet), the Trojan Horse, and the goddess Venus. One film, *Unico in the Island of Magic*, even features zombie-like dolls (or Living Puppets as they're called).

Charlie the Unicorn

Probably the silliest of all the unicorns in today's pop culture, Charlie captured the imaginations of millions of viewers who first saw him on YouTube in 2006. Amateur animator Jason Steele created the lazy and curmudgeonly unicorn, who along with his two annoying buddies (one pink, one blue), travels to the legendary Candy Mountain. When they reach their destination, however, Charlie gets trapped in a cave and loses consciousness. He wakes up in a grassy meadow, only to discover that his sleazy companions have ripped off one of his kidneys. The nonsensical short film turned out to be so popular that three sequels resulted between 2008 and 2012. As *Time* magazine summed it up, "*Charlie the Unicorn* proves that something doesn't have to make any sense at all to earn a cult following."

The list of pop unicorns goes on and on. From the saccharine-y sweet to the grossly ugly, unicorns turn up everywhere in our contemporary culture. For thousands of years, people revered these sublime creatures for their beauty, power, and goodness. Today, however, we've tucked our tongues firmly in our cheeks and interpreted this once-sacrosanct beast in a humorous and playful manner.

IT'S A GIRL THING

As we've seen in the previous chapters, myths and folklore have always connected unicorns with young women and girls. Today the girls who love unicorns tend to be much younger than those of the early legends—merchandisers aim unicorn products at preschoolers and even toddlers. Maybe that's because it's getting harder and harder these days to find virgins beyond a certain age.

Why Do Girls Love Unicorns?

Why does an innocent virgin choose to sit in the woods all alone, waiting for a unicorn to show up? Granted, the rare and lovely creature might make a pretty pet, but so would a Himalayan kitten. Most of the old tales don't consider why a young maiden might want to befriend a unicorn, probably because in earlier times nobody much cared what girls thought or wanted anyway.

Nina Shen Rastogi's article "Why Do Girls Love Unicorns? It's More Than Just the Horn," published on National Public Radio's website in February 2011, looks at the story from the girl's point of view. We all know that only a virgin female can tame a unicorn—and for women and girls who historically lacked any real power in their everyday world, it's got to be pretty intoxicating to win over such a wild, independent beast when nobody else can.

But it's not just about power. We all long to be loved and valued. As Rastogi explains, "I think for many young girls, there's a fantasy that someday you will be recognized as the secretly beautiful, magical thing that you are. The unicorn will be attracted to something ineffable about you, secret from the rest of the world."

Some sources, however, question the concept of marketing unicorns to little girls—some of them still in diapers. Although today's unicorns hardly resemble the fiercely independent and majestic creatures of old—they've been watered down to make them as palatable to kids as apple juice—the horned beast still symbolizes male power and fertility. Critics ask, what messages are we giving girl toddlers when we send them off to bed with these phallic toys? Others wonder about the denatured images of masculinity that we're presenting to children. Are the critics' concerns valid, or much ado about nothing?

Modern-Day Masculinity and the Unicorn

According to Bud Harris, PhD, author of *Resurrecting the Unicorn: Masculinity in the 21st Century,* the way the unicorn is envisioned at any given time period provides insight into the state of masculinity in that particular period's culture. During the medieval and Renaissance eras, for example, when a knight in shining armor represented the ideal man, the unicorn displayed characteristics of strength, loyalty, courage, chivalry, independence, and purity. In the twenty-first century, however, Harris says our sense of masculinity has become "impoverished." He claims the powerful, creative spirit that once infused men—or at least our image of what a man should be—is "sputtering out," and we see that change echoed in our depictions of the unicorn.

Certainly, the candy-colored, soft and plushy unicorn toys and the cartoon characters that prance across our TV and movie screens give no inkling of the magic, mystery, and total awesomeness that once surrounded a unicorn. In fact, few people today even connect the unicorn with men—we think of it as a girl thing. "The unicorn, that wondrous masculine symbol, has been reduced to a limp-horned stuffed animal found in novelty stores—or worse yet, discarded to a dusty old shelf of a second-hand thrift shop," Harris laments.

Does the unicorn serve as a barometer for the tenor of the times? A reflection of our psycho-sexual-spiritual attitudes? If I were a guy, I'd sure hate to look in a mirror and see the bloated *Despicable Me* unicorn staring back. Or is our present-day approach just fun and games, a reaction to the seriousness of previous generations of unicorn lovers?

Unicorns in Gay Culture

In his 2013 column "Rainbows and Unicorns: A Linguistic History" for *The Week*, Neil Whitman presented a graph that shows a steady increase in the popularity of unicorns, rainbows, and butterflies since 2003. Whitman also noted that the Zandl Group, a New York-based agency that tracks lifestyle trends, "puts the increasing popularity of rainbows and unicorns in the context of the mainstreaming of gay cultural symbols." Zandl goes on to say, "Pop culture has started to embrace and find humorous irony in gay iconography, symbolism and culture, without coming across as derogatory or un-PC."

Unicorns for Boys and Girls

When the animated TV show *My Little Pony: Friendship Is Magic* first aired in October 2010, the marketing folks noticed something unexpected in the viewer demographics. Not only were young girls watching the program, the audience also included a sizable number of males.

Why has the unicorn become associated with gay culture? Obviously, the horn is a factor, but that's not the only reason. Traditionally, legends have portrayed the unicorn as a rare, independent, and untamed creature that doesn't subscribe to the ordinary rules of conventional society—and certainly some parallels exist there. The theme of the unicorn befriending the virgin girl may also apply, not along the lines of early Christian interpretation, but as representing two sectors of society who have been unappreciated historically simply on the basis of sex.

Unicorn Shoes

So far as we know, nobody has fabricated shoes from actual unicorn hide—animal rights organizations would jump all over that. However, the unicorn has served as an inspiration for fashion designers, including Jeffrey Campbell. When introduced in 2009, Campbell's "Unicorn Princess Heels" with quirky, corkscrew high heels reminiscent of a unicorn's horn created a buzz in the fashion world and delighted not only virgins, but vixens as well. If high heels aren't your thing, you can still tap the trend by lacing on sneakers decorated with pictures of unicorns and rainbows.

LET THE GAMES BEGIN

The unicorn was among the first characters in the Dungeons & Dragons menagerie back in the mid-1970s when the game first burst on the scene. Based on traditional mythology, the D&D unicorn possessed magical ability and resembled a beautiful white horse with the usual spiral-shaped horn in the middle of its forehead. The unicorn's temperament and behavior also followed the legends: it was reclusive, intuitive, and long-lived. Maiden warriors could control and even ride the unicorn, which meant the creature naturally fell into the category of nice guys in the game. By the early nineties, a number of different colors and variations had evolved, including a faerie unicorn, a sea unicorn, and a zebracorn—even a corrupt and evil version, known as a Shadow Unicorn (see C.G. Jung's work for insight into "shadows").

Unicorns the Gaming World

Since then, the unicorn has starred in lots of computer and board games for boys, girls, and adults. "Crypt Worlds," for instance, features a low-res and homely Unicorn Goddess who's trying to retrieve magical artifacts in order to save the world. Players can choose to help her protect the world from evil by marking their territory—or not. In "The Elder Scrolls IV: Oblivion," the unicorn is portrayed as an aggressive character that attacks with its horn. "Overlord" depicts unicorns as bloodthirsty beasts, and you have to kill them before they kill you. "Fantasy Quest"'s unicorns love carrots and "NetHacks" can be tempted with gemstones. In "Dragon Age: Inquisition" the creepy Bog Unicorn is a zombie horse with a sword in its head instead of a horn.

"Robot Unicorn Attack" from Adult Swim, which turned up on several of Apple's best games lists, is aimed at young men in the twenty-to-thirty age bracket, but it includes lots of tongue-in-cheek girlie goofiness. The object is to navigate your unicorn through a glittery universe, using your rainbow power.

Games for girls usually dispense with the fantasy universes, wars, and violence typical of boys' games. Instead, they invite players to use their creativity to alter the appearances of basic unicorns—an updated version of dressing up dolls. Girls can change the unicorns' body colors and mane styles, give them Pegasus wings, alter their horns, and adorn them with necklaces, anklets, saddles, or Mardi Gras-style masks. My Little Pony offers fans a collection of unicorn games that draw on old favorites, such as matching shapes, remembering objects, and guessing what's behind closed doors.

> *"[U]nicorns can thrive anywhere that the heart and imagination are receptive to them."*
>
> —Paul and Karin Johnsgard,
> *Dragons and Unicorns: A Natural History*

Raise Your Own Unicorns

Want to raise your own unicorns and pegacorns—even a phoenix pegacorn? The game, named "Unicorn Island," lets you play rancher and establish your herd, er, *glory*, in a fantasy community that the game's designers dubbed Farmville (although it probably should have a cool dude ranch-type name because, really, farms are where you raise chickens and cabbages). When you get enough animals in your pens, you can "harvest" them in return for gemstones. As you can see from a quick glance at the amazing array of unicorn products on the market today, raising them can be a very lucrative business venture with virtually no limitations. (Given that the powers-that-be don't even believe unicorns exist, you can fly beneath the radar when it comes to licenses, permits, zoning, and all that stuff.)

Just to make sure you've got the fundamentals of Unicornomics down, you'll want to consult Jessica Marquis's whimsical step-by-step guide *Raising Unicorns: Your Step-by-Step Guide to Starting and Running a Successful—and Magical!—Unicorn Farm*. It provides all the information you need to know about planning your strategy and developing your business plan, understanding unicorn magic and hazards, and expanding your operation. And making dreams come true, too—that's important. Marquis answers your questions on *www.unicornomics.com,* such as what to feed a fussy unicorn and how to prevent your unicorns from bumping their horns on Plexiglas ceilings (they can break through glass ceilings).

Chances are good that the unicorn hasn't seen its last game. Its magic and mystery, as well as its beauty, make it simply too intriguing for game creators to resist. Besides, you've got to have a good character in there along with all those monsters and villains—and who could better fill the role?

Unicorn Aliases

Now you can get your very own unicorn alias, by visiting The Unicorn Name Generator (*http://unicorn.namegeneratorfun.com*). The site generates a unique unicorn-themed moniker for you to use for role-playing games or just for fun. It also describes your personality as a unicorn. For example, Brad Pitt's unicorn name is Windy Velvet Saddle, and he's described as "silly and lovable. He has a nose as soft as a kitten, and he brings happy dreams and sweet sleep."

BLENDING PEGASUS WITH THE UNICORN

What do you call a unicorn with wings? A Pegacorn? A Unipeg? The real question is, how did this mythic hybrid creature come about in the first place? And what's its purpose in our world today?

The Myth of Pegasus

In Greek mythology, the immortal winged horse Pegasus was the offspring of the sea god Poseidon and the gorgon Medusa. Medusa had been a beautiful woman, but when she became a gorgon her hair turned to snakes, and any person who looked her in the eye was instantly turned to stone. When the hero Perseus cut off mean old Medusa's snaky head, the beautiful Pegasus sprang from her blood. The creature got its horsey shape from his father, who had shapeshifted into a horse in order to seduce Medusa.

The ancient Greeks thought Pegasus's wings were made of ground unicorn horn and only the goddess Athena could tame the magical flying horse. In case you're not familiar with her, the wise and talented Athena wasn't your ordinary girl next door. First of all, she emerged fully grown from Zeus's head, instead of being born in the usual manner. Second, she's generally considered a warrior-protector figure armed with a spear and shield, as well as an ethical deity whose purity and upstanding character were beyond question. Although she hasn't gone down in history as a notable virgin, like her Olympian counterpart Artemis, she possesses qualities that might endear her to a unicorn as well as Pegasus.

Similarities Between Pegasus and the Unicorn

Pegasus and the unicorn have some similarities, which, in a sense, could make them buddies in the mythic realm. For instance:

- Both are gentle beings who symbolize freedom, joy, innocence, and kindness.
- Both are incredibly beautiful, and usually depicted as pure white.
- Both have the ability to provide life-giving water to those who thirst (that's another metaphor for another time). Pegasus strikes rocks with his hoof to bring forth fountains, whereas the unicorn immerses his horn in bodies of water to cleanse them of impurities. Legend also tells us that the unicorn jabbed his horn into a rock and water spewed from it.

Maybe it's not so strange to think that the two creatures might become merged into a single entity. Assyrian seals dating back to the eighth century show winged unicorns, and the Chinese unicorn is usually pictured with wings. We even have quite a few animal cross-species on earth already: the mule (the offspring of a horse and a donkey), the liger (a lion-tiger cross), and the camas (a camel-llama blend). Why not a pegacorn?

According to Candace N. Coonan in her book *Where Shadows Linger*, "Once there were three breeds—the Pegasus, the Unicorn and a mix of the two, which were regarded as a unique group. During the War of the Trees, all the Unicorns fled Alexandria, leaving the Pegasus-Unicorns as their only legacy."

Breeding a Better Beast?

Contemporary culture has seamlessly merged the two mythological creatures and come up with a fanciful being that embodies the best of both. Although these two magnificent beasts have many similarities, each brings to the pairing a quality that the other lacks. Pegasus's wings, for instance, enable him to rise above earth's trials and tribulations, and to soar into the heavens. Additionally, his divine parentage links him with the higher worlds, so he's sort of like an angel. The unicorn's horn suggests the ability to fight when necessary, to take a stand for what he believes, and to marshal a defense against the forces of evil here on earth.

From a psychological perspective, unicorns symbolize delving deep within yourself to discover your hidden strengths. The forest where the unicorn lives signifies the dark and convoluted territory of the subconscious. Its spiral horn, which protrudes from the third eye or psychic center, represents using your intuition as well as your intellect. Pegasus symbolizes spiritual questing in order to connect with the deities who, legends tell us, preside over the mundane world. It also urges you to set your sights high—the sky's the limit.

Put together, the two form an amazing entity that's strong and sensitive, protective and loyal, earthy and spiritual. And beautiful, of course. No wonder women love it!

Pegacorns in Pop Culture

Hasbro's Princess Twilight Sparkle isn't the only modern-day pegacorn to break into pop culture. Barbie's Secret Door series features one, too. Ty's Beanie Babies collection also boasts one in its plushy stables. In *Princess Gwenevere and the Jewel Riders*, an animated TV series from the mid-1990s that borrows from the Arthurian legends, young Gwen rides Sunstar, a white-and-pink winged unicorn with a golden mane and tail. "The Last Winged Unicorn" from Horse Games lets you jump, er, fly your pegacorn over obstacles with a click of your keyboard.

But winged unicorns aren't new kids on the block. They date back to ancient Rome, where the philosopher Pliny the Elder referred to them in his first-century text *Natural History*. Pliny thought the rare and awe-inspiring creatures were the real deal and could be found in Ethiopia. But he didn't envision them as the gorgeous beings we think of today—he described them as monstrosities. Pegacorns were also pictured in some of the early bestiaries (see Chapter 5) and in medieval art. Purists may balk at the idea, but the fact is, the pegacorn or unipeg or whatever you want to call it has been around for a long, long time—and it's here to stay.

Unicorns in the Business World

The business world has co-opted the unicorn and its symbolism—most notably the creature's rarity—and linked it with big-bucks companies. In today's corporate lexicon, the term "unicorn" refers to a company that's valued at more than $1 billion. Posting on TechCrunch's site (*www.techcrunch.com*) in 2013, Aileen Lee, founder of Cowboy Ventures, identified thirty-nine technology companies (going back to 2003) that she dubbed "The Unicorn Club," which fall into this "rare breed" category. As Lee pointed out, however, the problem with unicorns is not only are they hard to find, but they don't always produce the profits their investors hope for. What to do? Go after an even rarer beast. According to John Backus, a founder of New Atlantic Ventures, in an article for TechCrunch, "Look beyond the unicorn and find the dragon. Unicorns are for show. Dragons are for dough."

UNICORN ART TODAY

Artists can't resist the unicorn. All the way back in prehistoric times, our cave-dwelling ancestors painted pictures of unicorns on the walls of their caves (see Chapter 4). Throughout history, unicorns have starred in paintings, sculptures, mosaics, and of course, the famous tapestries of the early Renaissance period. Noted artists from Leonardo da Vinci to Salvador Dalí have depicted their visions of unicorns. Some represent the fabled creatures as exquisitely lovely; others show them as peculiar, to say the least. The unicorn's allure is as great for artists today as it was centuries ago. A quick tour of Etsy will turn up all manner of unicorn art, from the cute to the kitschy to the surreal, along with unicorn-printed T-shirts, jewelry, phone cases, and eye charts.

Even some of the world's most renowned contemporary artists, galleries, and museums find the unicorn juicy subject matter. Take, for instance, Thomas Woodruff's interpretation of the Unicorn Tapestries titled *Landscape Variation: Sanguinic*, exhibited in 2012 at the P•P•O•W Gallery in New York City. It features a pink pegacorn with not just the usual single horn spiraling out from the animal's forehead, but three decorative other horns as well. The colorful creature stands in a landscape blossoming profusely with fuchsia and red roses, while a pink lady perched in a bouquet plays the unicorn's primary horn like a flute.

Kathy Ruttenberg's ceramic sculpture *Careful What You Wish For* shows a woman with a unicorn's head standing like an acrobat on the back of a horse. Saint Clair Cemin's *Lincorne* follows in the footsteps of the sixteenth-century Italian artist Benvenuto Cellini (see Chapter 6). In 2006, Saint Clair Cemin fashioned a bronze unicorn's head to serve as the base for a swirling narwhal's tusk owned by the Musée de la Chasse et de la Nature in Paris. German sculptor Rebecca Horn (playing on her own surname) recalls the unicorn's link to chastity with her strap-on *Einhorn*, designed to wear in performance art; it's now part of the Tate's collection. For *The Dream*, Englishman Damien Hirst attached a horn to an actual pure-white colt and placed it in a display case filled with a formaldehyde solution.

Despite centuries of portraying the magical and elusive unicorn in art of all kinds, the fact remains that no one really knows what the beast actually looks like. And that opens the doors for artists in the future to continue imagining and interpreting the unicorn for the rest of us to enjoy.

The Ten Silliest Unicorn Products

It's hard to narrow down the plethora of kitsch and craziness out there to just ten truly silly products. A quick online search turns up scores of ludicrous items aimed at unicorn fans, from the laughable, to the idiotic, to the downright disgusting. You can purchase everything from your own full-size latex unicorn head mask (for those days when you really would prefer to be a unicorn) to sex toys that mimic the distinctive spiral-shaped horn—and a whole bunch of other stuff you probably never would have imagined existed.

Here's a short list of some whacky wonders for that person who has everything:

1. Unicorn fetuses in laboratory bottles, made by Spanish artist Soraya Merino

2. Canned Unicorn Meat, from Radiant Farms, contains a dismembered stuffed toy unicorn (no, it's not edible)

3. A singing unicorn toothbrush that teaches kids how to brush properly, from Pillow Pets

4. An inflatable unicorn horn for your cat, with chin strap, from Totally Funky (its makers insist your cat will love it, but I wouldn't bet on that)

5. Uni-corn Corn Holders (for corn on the cob), in assorted colors, from BaronBob.com

6. Long Winter Farm Unicorn Farts in a Tube, from Long Winter Soap Co. (it's actually lip balm)

7. Unicorn Poop chewing gum in rainbow colors, from BaronBob.com

8. A plush Unicorn Bouquet of a dozen tiny unicorns in pink, aqua, and purple, from ThinkGeek—who needs roses?

9. Unicorn Milk vapor flavor (ejuice) that tastes like strawberry milk, from Cuttwood

10. Unicorn Tears silly putty, from ThinkGeek

As society continues to evolve, so will unicorns. They've been with us for millennia, reflecting not only our changing cultural, religious, and political ideas, but also our hopes and dreams—and it's a pretty safe bet that unicorns will stick around for a while longer. Today's unicorn enthusiasts are pushing the outside of the envelope, shepherding the beast into previously uncharted territory, both ridiculous and sublime. Yet even the goofiest goods and gadgets indicate a fascination with the fanciful creature—and maybe an entrepreneurial spirit, like that of the alicorn purveyors of yore.

Then, Now, and Beyond: The Evolution of Unicorns

"(O)ur understanding of the unicorn hasn't changed for over 2000 years. It has traveled across continents and gotten lost in translation, but has never disappeared. It is perhaps the most commonly-seen uncommon animal in the history of the world."

—Annalee Newitz,
"The Bizarre History of Our Obsession with Unicorns"

DURING THE COURSE of this book, we've journeyed with the unicorn through time, from prehistory to the present. We've witnessed many of the interpretations people around the world have ascribed to this most magical and mysterious creature. We've seen how cultural, political, religious, and economic forces have influenced our ideas about the unicorn in the past and continue to do so today. Despite changes in our mundane world, however, the mystical unicorn has remained a most enchanting and beloved entity in the minds of young and old alike.

Along the way, we've considered whether or not the beautiful beast is now or was ever a real, flesh-and-blood animal that graced earth with its noble presence. Certainly our ancestors thought so. Plenty of reports from reliable sources testify to the fact that unicorns may have lived among us in bygone eras, and perhaps still do. Sightings, though rare, support the belief that at least a few lucky people have been privileged to view unicorns. Researchers have even managed to produce a few one-horned animals that resulted from quirks of nature or human intervention, animals that might have inspired our early conceptions of the elusive creature.

For many of us, this evidence is enough. Many of the rest of us don't care if unicorns ever made an appearance on Planet Earth— their mystique is part of their appeal. As Terry Brooks points out in *The Black Unicorn*, "After all there has to be some belief in magic— however small—for any world to survive."

"*Should the last of the gentle unicorns also perish, they will continue to haunt our dreams and those of our children, who will not forgive us for letting such beauty disappear from the earth.*"

—Paul and Karin Johnsgard, *Dragons and Unicorns: A Natural History*

Perhaps the unicorn abides in a parallel universe that connects with our own, maybe via time-warp portals or magic wardrobes. Or it might live in a nonphysical realm as a spirit being. Because its energetic resonance isn't the same as that of human beings, we don't usually see it. Like ghosts, fairies, mermaids, Bigfoot, ETs, and other entities we can't explain, the unicorn occasionally shifts its vibration—or we shift ours—so that we're both on the same wavelength temporarily. When that happens, we catch a glimpse of the magnificent creature and it dazzles us. We can't stop thinking about it, talking about it, longing for it. In an attempt to recapture its fleeting image, we paint pictures, write stories, and tell tales around campfires and kitchen tables about the wonder we've witnessed.

The amazing unicorn of myth probably isn't and never was a physical being. That's why anthropologists and archaeologists have never unearthed any unicorn bones or ribbed horns as proof of its authenticity. However, they've never proved it *didn't* exist, either. But the truth is, it doesn't matter.

"Unicorn sings ravishing melodies for those who possess the inner ear of mystics and poets. . . . And he haunts those ivory gates of sleep whence come ineffable dreams to mortals. . . .
We must believe in the reality of our Unicorn."

—James Huneker, *Unicorns*

THE UNICORN'S ENDURING LEGACY

What the unicorn means to us, what the myths and legends about it teach us, are more important than whether or not such a beast actually trod our planet with its cloven hooves. Throughout history, the unicorn has always represented the forces of good. It's given us hope and enchanted us with its beauty. The unicorn, Megan Lindholm says in "The Unicorn in the Maze," "was a marvelous beast, shining with honor, wisdom and strength. Just to see him strengthened the soul."

Let's take a final look at some of the key characteristics we associate with the unicorn and what we can learn from it:

- Unicorns symbolize peace. You'll never see a unicorn playing road rage games or shooting up a convenience store or bombing a village. Like beacons in the night, unicorns shine a light in the darkness. They show humans how to behave better and stop hurting each other.
- Unicorns represent honor, strength, and virtue. You'll never see a unicorn picking on someone weaker than itself—instead, they take care of the innocent and in some

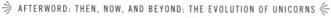

cases punish the wicked. From them we can learn compassion for those less fortunate than ourselves, kindness toward the young and the old, honesty in our dealings with others, and respect for all the earth's inhabitants.

- Unicorns embody independence. You'll never see a unicorn kowtowing to bogus authority or cozying up to someone with influence. These noble creatures stand on their own merit and follow their own truth. By emulating them, we can learn to stand on our own two feet and be responsible for our actions. We won't lean on others or let them manipulate us, nor will we buy into propaganda or sacrifice our principles for personal gain.
- Unicorns behave modestly. You'll never see a unicorn boasting in a bar or grabbing the spotlight or trying to get ahead at someone else's expense. Unicorns know they're hands down the most exquisite creatures ever, and they needn't prove themselves to anyone. Watching them can help us to value ourselves and appreciate our unique talents.
- Unicorns are loyal and devoted to those they love. You'll never see a unicorn cheating on its mate or abandoning its children or leaving town when the going gets tough. Like the chivalrous knights in medieval times, unicorns teach us to honor our commitments and the people to whom we've pledged ourselves. By following in their footsteps, er, hoof prints, we can become more discerning and wise in our choices of companions; we can recognize true love instead of selling ourselves short in matters of the heart.

"[T]here have never been Unicorn Riots, Unicorn Wars, Unicorn Persecutions, Unicorn Plagues, Unicorn Famines. A scholar in his study studying unicorns will encompass no one's death in the sacred names of Science and Technology. Perhaps we are where we are because we have no more unicorns."

—Avram Davidson, "The Spoor of the Unicorn"

THE FUTURE OF UNICORNS

Does anybody want to speculate on what unicorns will look like twenty years from now? Or in the next century? The previous chapters in this book have shown how our conceptions of unicorns have changed over the years. We've seen unicorns shift from untamed and powerful beings to cuddly playmates for children. One thing we know from observing history is that the pendulum always swings from one extreme to the other. What's "in" today will be "out" tomorrow.

My guess is that the future will restore the unicorn to its earlier grandeur. The wild, brave, and solitary unicorn who inspired awe and reverence in our ancestors was never meant to line the aisles of Toys "R" Us or poop rainbows on your T-shirt. Nor did his lofty aspirations include perching as an ornament on the hood of your car or being tattooed on your backside. The childish cuteness and sophomoric silliness with which we've interpreted the unicorn in recent years will fade away, like a once trendy Hollywood star who's become passé. One day, we will again focus on his majesty and mystical nature. He may still deign to lay his head in your adolescent daughter's lap and let her pat his silken neck, but he won't stand still for her to slap a pink saddle on his back or paint nail polish on his hooves.

"If we are to learn anything from dragons and unicorns, it is that animals should not be judged by human values—that is, whether they are useful to us or whether or not they conform to our own ideas of beauty. There is a place for unicorns in this world, just as there is a place for dragons, and if we do not allow both these creatures to survive and prosper in some form, we can hold out little hope for our own survival."

—Paul and Karin Johnsgard, *Dragons and Unicorns: A Natural History*

No matter what, I suspect that the unicorn will always be with us. He might retreat deep into the forest in order to escape all the hoopla surrounding him today, and we may have to look harder and be more sincere in the future if we want to find him. But we'll continue searching for this Holy Grail of the animal world just as we have for millennia, and, ultimately, I believe that we'll find his glory deep within ourselves.

Bibliography

Aelian. *On the Characteristics of Animals*. Ed. and trans. by A.F. Scholfield. 3 vols. Loeb Classical Library. (London: Heinemann, 1958).

Alexander, Skye. *The Secret Power of Spirit Animals* (Avon, Mass.: Adams Media, 2013).

_____. *Mermaids: The Myths, Legends, & Lore*. (Avon, Mass.: Adams Media, 2012).

_____. *Fairies: The Myths, Legends, & Lore*. (Avon, Mass.: Adams Media, 2014).

Andrews, Ted. *Treasures of the Unicorn: The Return to the Sacred Quest*. (Batabia, Ohio: Dragonhawk Publishing, 1996).

Aristotle. *History of Animals*. Ed. and trans. by Richard Cresswell. (London: George Bell and Sons, 1883).

Aunt Naomi. *Jewish Fairy Tales and Legends*. (New York: Bloch Publishing, Inc., 1919).

Baring-Gould, William S. and Ceil. *The Annotated Mother Goose*. (New York: Meridian, 1967).

Barnes, Albert Rev. *Notes, critical, illustrative, and practical on the Book of Job*, Vol. II (London: George Routledge, 1847).

Beagle, Peter S. *The Last Unicorn*. (New York: Viking Press, 1968).

_____. "Julie's Unicorn" in *The Rhinoceros Who Quoted Nietzsche*. (San Francisco: Tachyon Publications, 1997).

Beagle, Peter S., Janet Berliner, and Martin H. Greenberg, Eds. *Peter S. Beagle's Immortal Unicorn*. (New York: HarperPrism, 1995).

Bingen, Hildegarde. *Physica*. Ed. and trans. by Priscilla Throop. (Rochester, Vt: Healing Arts Press, 1998).

Bittel, Jason. "Real-Life 'Unicorn' Found; Deer Has Extremely Rare Deformity." *National Geographic*, November 12, 2014.

Black, Holly and Larbalestier, Justine, Eds. *Zombies vs. Unicorns*. (New York: Margaret K. McElderry Books, 2010).

Bradley, Josephine. *In Pursuit of the Unicorn*. (Portland, Ore.: Pomegranate Art Books, 1980).

Brooks, Terry. *The Black Unicorn*. (New York: Del Ray, 1987).

Brown, Robert. *The Unicorn: A Mythological Investigation*. (London: Spottswoode & Co., 1881).

Carroll, Lewis. *Alice's Adventures in Wonderland & Through the Looking-Glass*. (New York: Bantam Classics, 1984).

Cellini, Benvenuto. *Autobiography*. (Cambridge, Mass.: The Harvard Classics, 1909–14). (*www.bartleby.com*)

Chevalier, Tracy. *The Lady and the Unicorn*. (New York: Plume, 2004).

Christie, Anthony. *Chinese Mythology*. (UK: Hamlyn Publishing Group Ltd., 1968).

Coonan, Candace N. *Where Shadows Linger*. (Trafford Publishing, 2012).

Coville, Bruce. *Into the Land of the Unicorns*. (New York: Scholastic Press, 1999).

_____. *Song of the Wanderer*. (New York: Scholastic Press, 1999).

_____. *Dark Whispers*. (New York: Scholastic Press, 2008).

_____. *The Last Hunt*. (New York: Scholastic Press, 2010).

_____. *A Glory of Unicorns*. (New York: Scholastic Press, 2000).

Dozois, Gardner and Dann, Jack, Eds. *Unicorns 1*. (Baen Books, 2013). (*www.baenebooks.com*).

Dudley, William. *Unicorns*. (San Diego: Reference Point Press, 2008).

Encyclopedia Britannica (www.britannica.com)

Forbes, V.S. *Anders Sparrman Travels in the Cape 1772–1776, Vol. II*. (Cape Town, South Africa: Van Riebeeck Society, 1977).

Freeman, Margaret B. *The Unicorn Tapestries*. (New York: The Metropolitan Museum of Art, 1976).

Gaiman, Neil and Vess, Charles. *Stardust*. (New York: Vertigo/D.C. Comics, 1998).

Gill, N.S. "Unicorns in Greece and Rome: Greek and Roman Literary Sources on the Unicorn." (*http://ancienthistory.about.com*)

Gould, Charles. *Mythological Monsters*. (London: W.H. Allen and Co., 1886).

Green, Michael. *De Historia et Veritate Unicornis: On the History and Truth of the Unicorn*. Translation supervised by James J. O'Donnell (Philadelphia: Running Press Book Publishers, 1983).

Grimm, Jacob and Wilhelm. *The Complete Fairy Tales of the Brothers Grimm*. Ed. and trans. by Jack Zipes. (New York: Bantam, 1987).

Harris, Bud, PhD. *Resurrecting the Unicorn: Masculinity in the 21st Century*. (Carmel, Calif.: Fisher King Press, 2008).

Hathaway, Nancy. *The Unicorn*. (New York: Random House, 1987).

Hoch, Edward D. "The Last Unicorns" in *100 Great Fantasy Short Short Stories*. Eds. Isaac Asimov, Terry Carr, and Martin H. Greenberg. (New York: Avon, 1984).

The Holy Bible. The King James Version. Ed. Thomas Nelson. (Nashville, Tenn.: 1986).

Huneker, James. *Unicorns* (New York: Charles Scribner's Sons, 1917).

Hyde, Walter Woodburn. "The Curious Animals of the Hercynian Forest," *The Classical Journal* Vol. 13, No. 4, January 1918. (*www.jstor.org*)

Johnsgard, Paul and Karin. *Dragons and Unicorns: A Natural History.* (New York: St. Martin's Press, 1982).

Lavers, Chris, PhD. *The Natural History of Unicorns.* (New York: HarperCollins, 2009).

Lee, Tanith. *Black Unicorn.* (England: Atheneum Books, 1991).

L'Engle, Madelaine. *A Swiftly Tilting Planet.* (New York: Square Fish, 2007).

Lewis, C.S. *The Chronicles of Narnia.* (New York: HarperCollins, 2001).

Lothlorien, Elle. *Alice in Wonderland.* (CreateSpace Independent Publishing Platform, 2013).

Marquis, Jessica S. *Raising Unicorns: Your Step-by-Step Guide to Starting and Running a Successful—and Magical—Unicorn Farm.* (Avon, Mass.: Adams Media, 2011).

Mayer, Marianna. *The Unicorn and the Lake.* Michael Hague, illustrator. (Children's Book-of-the-Month Club, 2005).

_____. *The Unicorn Alphabet.* Michael Hague, illustrator. (New York: Dial Books, 1998).

McCaughrean, Geraldine. *Unicorns! Unicorns!* (New York: Holiday House, 1997).

McHargue, Georgess. *The Beasts Of Never.* (Indianapolis: Bobbs Merrill Co., 1968).

McLeish, Todd. *Narwhals: Arctic Whales in a Melting World.* (Seattle, Wash.: University of Washington Press, 2013).

McNamee, Gregory. *Aelian's On the Nature of Animals.* (San Antonio, Texas: Trinity University Press, 2011).

Murray, Christopher John, Ed. *Encyclopedia of the Romantic Era, 1760–1850.* (New York: Fitzroy Dearborn, 2004).

Newman, Sharan. *Guinevere.* (New York: St. Martin's Press, 1981).

Niven, Larry. *The Flight of the Horse.* (New York: Del Ray, 1977).

Ortner, Sherry B. "The Virgin and the State." *Feminist Studies* 4.3 (1978): 19–35. *JSTOR*. Web. 17 Apr. 2013.

Peterfreund, Diana. *Rampant.* (New York: HarperCollins, 2009.)

_____. *Errant.* (New York: HarperTeen, 2012).

_____. *Ascendant.* (Word for Word, 2013).

Physiologus. Ed. and trans. by Michael J. Curley. (Chicago: University of Chicago Press, 2009).

Pilinovsky, Helen, PhD. "The Unicorn Tapestries and Other Depictions: Beyond the Obvious Symbolism of the Unicorn's Horn," *Fantasy* Issue 58, October 2014 (*www.fantasy-magazine.com*).

Preston, Richard. "Capturing the Unicorn" *The New Yorker*, April 11, 2005.

Princely Splendor: The Dresden Court 1580–1620, Dirk Syndram and Antje Scherner, Eds. (Dresden, Germany: Staatliche Kunstammlungen Dresden, 2004).

Rabelais, Francois. *Gargantua and Pantagruel*. Ed. and trans. by Sir Thomas Urquhart and Peter le Motteux. (London: David Nutt, 1900).

Rampton, Martha. "The Three Waves of Feminism," *Pacific*, October 23, 2014, Pacific University Oregon (*www.pacificu.edu*).

Rastogi, Nina Shen. "Why Do Girls Love Unicorns? It's More Than Just the Horn," *Slate*, February 9, 2011 (*www.npr.org*).

Rowling, J.K. *Harry Potter and the Sorcerer's Stone*. (New York: Scholastic Press, 1998).

Shakespeare, William. *The Riverside Shakespeare*. (New York: Houghton Mifflin, 1996).

Shepard, Odell. *The Lore of the Unicorn*. (London: George Allen & Unwin; Boston: Houghton Mifflin, 1930).

Singer, Irving. *The Nature of Love*. (Cambridge, Mass.: The MIT Press, 2009).

Spenser, Edmund. *Edmund Spenser's Poetry*. (New York: W.W. Norton, 1993).

"The unicorn and its mythology: The Cloisters marks its 75th anniversary with a celebration of the unicorn," *The Economist*, June 15, 2013 (*www.economist.com*).

"The Unicorn and the Mermaid," *Blackwood's Edinburgh Magazine*, No. LXVI, Vol. XII, July 1822.

Thurber, James. *The Thurber Carnival*. (New York: Harper and Brothers, 1945).

Vajracharya, Gautama V. "Unicorns in Ancient India and Vedic Ritual," *Electronic Journal of Vedic Studies* (EJVS) Vol. 17, Issue 2, 2010 (*www.ejvs.laurasianacademy.com*).

Von Bingen, Hildegard. Trans. Priscilla Throop. *Hildegard von Bingen's Physica: The Complete English Translation of Her Classic Work on Health and Healing*. (Rochester, Vt.: Healing Arts Press, 1998).

Wilhelm, Richard and Baynes, Cary F. *The I Ching or Book of Changes*. (New York: Bollingen Foundation, Inc., 1950).

Williams, Tennessee. *The Glass Menagerie*. (1944).

White, T.H. *The Once and Future King*. (New York: Ace Books, 1987).

Wolfe, Gene. "The Woman the Unicorn Loved." *Issac Asimov's Science Fiction Magazine*, June 1980.

Zelazny, Roger. *Unicorn Variations.* (UK: Sphere Books, 1985).

_____. *The Great Book of Amber.* (New York: Avon Eos, 1999).

Zell-Ravenheart, Oberon. "Creature of the Month—The Unicorn," June 23, 2011, (*http://newpagebooks.blogspot.com/2011/06/creature-of-month-unicorn-by-oberon.html*).

Online Resources

The Aberdeen Bestiary Project, University of Aberdeen, UK, *www.abdn.ac.uk/bestiary*

www.about.com

www.allaboutunicorns.com

www.amnh.org

www.angelfire.com

http://archive.library.yale.edu

www.artblart.com

www.artnews.com

www.baenebooks.com

http://bestiary.ca/intro.htm

www.biography.com

http://britishlibrary.typepad.co.uk

www.brucecoville.com

http://carljungdepthpsychology.blogspot.com

www.dartmouth.edu

www.dianapeterfreund.com

www.economist.com

www.fantasy-magazine.com

www.ginadianneharding.com

http://globalwarming-arclein.blogspot.com

www.gods-and-monsters.com

www.goodreads.com

www.gutenberg.org

www.hasbro.com

www.history.com

www.historyofpainters.com

http://ia801408.us.archive.org

www.imdb.com

www.io9.com

www.killerunicorns.org

www.livingartsoriginals.com

www.malindalo.com

http://mammothtales.blogspot.com

www.mentalfloss.com

http://mythologyofchina.blogspot.com
www.nationalgeographic.com
www.newadvent.org
www.novareinna.com
www.occultopedia.com
http://omc.bc.edu/newarcadiacontent
www.ppowgallery.com
www.reuters.com
www.richmondscots.org
www.sacred-texts.com
www.stevewinick.com
www.symbolreader.net
www.tchevalier.com
www.techcrunch.com

www.tvtropes.org
www.ultimatehorsesite.com
www.unicorn-dream.co.uk
www.unicorngarden.com
http://unicorn.namegeneratorfun.com
www.urbandictionary.com
www.vietnamheritagetravel.com
www.thewhitegoddess.co.uk
www.theworldofchinese.com
Whitall, Austin. "Patagonian
   monsters," November 2009 (*http://*
   patagoniamonsters.blogspot.com)
www.youtube.com

Index

About the Author

SKYE ALEXANDER is the award-winning author of more than thirty fiction and nonfiction books, including *Mermaids: The Myths, Legends, & Lore*; *Fairies: The Myths, Legends, & Lore*; and *The Secret Power of Spirit Animals*. Her stories have been published in anthologies internationally, and her work has been translated into more than a dozen languages. She divides her time between Texas and Massachusetts.